最齊全的商務╳留學英文 **E-mail** 情境，

現在開始，

寫 **E-mail** 不再需要想半天！

使用說明

學習小撇步①

信件範本中英文對照,語句逐字查找一目瞭然

書中信件範本皆以單篇中英文上下對照排版而成,便於閱讀及中英語句之對照,不管想要只閱讀英文,測試自己的英文閱讀能力,或者閱讀中文翻譯,試著猜猜看這句話用英文可以怎麼說,只要有中英對照都不是問題。

學習小撇步②

每個主題附兩種版本答覆範本,鞏固學習廣度

本書列舉廣泛主題,讓在職場和準備出國留學的學習者可以根據自身需求找到對應的篇章學習、套用範本,針對該情境中發問的題目發想兩種可能出現的答覆,讓學習的層面可以更加完整。

學習小撇步③

聚焦精選主題常用焦點單字,寫信回信更精準

談論特定主題時,一定會出現使用頻率相對高於其他單字的字,為了避免書到用時方恨少的詞窮狀況,一定要率先學習這些精選單字!為了更加熟悉單字用法,這個區塊中還編寫了對應的例句。

　　撰寫正式商務往來及出國留學相關的 email 時，有許多需要注意的細節。

　　每一封 email 都會有目的及其想達成的具體目標，本書根據撰寫者的不同目的，針對該情境做可能出現的答覆的發想，為的是希望在遇到不同的情況時，若讀者有不同的回答，或許可以從書中範本中學習該怎麼寫。

　　例如，收到詢問商品價格運費的信時，可能會需要報價給對方，當然也可能出現因為無法提供折扣、免運費，而需要婉拒來信方的狀況。而本書在每一篇當中皆附上兩種版本的答覆，用意就在此：為了因應不同情況下產生的可能需要的回應。

　　透過閱讀貼近生活、主題廣泛、用字淺白的範本，相信在學習書寫 email 的過程中會減輕一些壓力，其實要寫好一封 email 並非難事，只要多看、多練習，寄出信件前多注意、多檢查，一定能夠有所進步。

目錄

Chepter 1 職場交流沒問題

Part 1 求職申請 Job applications

Part 2 處理訂單 Processing orders

Part 3 疑難雜症 Common situations

Part 4 發布通知 Notifications

Part 5 社交邀請 Social invitations

Part 6 恭喜祝賀 Congratulations

Part 7 職位變更 Personnel change

Chepter 2 出國留學萬事通

Chapter 1
職場交流沒問題

Unit 01 | 主動應徵信件

想**主動應徵**時，該怎麼寫呢？ ─ □ ✕

Dear Mr. Young,

My name is Jeffrey Hanz. I am particularly interested in your opening position of website **editor**; hence, I would like to apply for the job. As you may read from my CV, my major is literature and mass communication in a top ranked university. I have been working in a very popular website as an editor for three years. I believe I am qualified for this position with my skills and knowledge in website editorial business.

For your reference, please find my CV with my detailed information in the attachment. Looking forward to hearing from you!

Jeffrey Hanz

親愛的楊先生：

我叫傑弗瑞・翰茲，我對貴公司的網站編輯職缺非常感興趣，所以我想申請該職位。如您將在我的履歷上看到的，我在大學主修文學與大眾傳播學，我已經在一個非常受歡迎的網站工作了三年。我相信憑藉我在網站編輯業務的知識和技能，我會是此職缺的合適人選。

僅供您參考，隨函附上我的個人履歷。期待您的回覆！

傑弗瑞・翰茲

Part 2
Part 3
Part 4
Part 5
Part 6
Part 7

收到**主動應徵**的信，該怎麼回呢？ — □ ✕

Dear Jeffrey,

Thanks for your **enthusiasm** for this job; your professional knowledge and former experience are **impressive**. I already passed your CV to our HR who's in charge of this recruitment.

I am waiting for your good news.

Yours sincerely,

Young

親愛的傑弗瑞：

感謝你對這份工作的熱情，你的專業知識和工作經驗令人印象深刻。我已將你的履歷轉交給負責這次招聘的人事部同事。

期待你的好消息。

真誠地，

楊

不同的答覆還可以怎麼回呢？ — □ ✕

Dear Mr.Hanz,

I'm sorry to inform you that we've already hired an editor yesterday. But considering your **relevant** experience, we'd like to offer you another position which we think is also suitable for you. Would you mind meeting us if you are interested?

Yours respectfully,

Young

漢斯先生:

非常遺憾，我們昨天已經雇用了一位網站編輯。但考慮到你以前的相關工作經驗，我們有另一個同樣適合你的職務可以提供給你。如果你感興趣的話，我們能抽空面談嗎？

真誠地，

楊

 **重點單字**記起來，寫信回信超精準

① **editor** n. 編者、編輯
Amy Lin is the editor-in-chief of the famous fashion magazine. →林艾咪是那本著名時尚雜誌的主編。

② **enthusiasm** n. 熱心、熱忱、熱情
He completed the research with great enthusiasm.
→他以極大的熱情完成了研究。

③ **impressive** adj. 感人的、令人深刻印象的
The performance was so impressive that I wanted to watch it again.
→這場表演令人印象深刻，讓我想再看一次。

④ **relevant** adj. 有關的、中肯的、有重大作用的
Your point is just not relevant here in the discussion.
→你的論點在現在的討論中真的不切合主題。

Unit 02 寫自我推薦信

想**自我推薦爭取面試機會**時，該怎麼寫呢？ — □ ✕

Dear Sir or Madam,

My name is Jude Kane. I read your **recruitment** advertisement for a system administrator on a recruitment website. As the opening seems very much alike to the career opportunity I am seeking now, I am sending this letter to apply for the position.

As you may read in my CV, I graduated from a **prestigious** university, with a bachelor degree major in computer science, and I have been working in a large software company for 2 years. I am confident that my **competence** can meet your requirements. I'm sincerely looking forward to an interview at your earliest **convenience**.

Jude Kane

尊敬的先生或女士：

您好！我的名字叫裘蒂‧凱恩。最近我在一個招聘網站上看到貴公司的系統管理員招聘廣告。由於這個職缺與我目前正在尋找的職業機會很吻合，特此寫了這封信申請該職位。

您可以從我的個人履歷中讀到，我畢業於一所頂尖大學，取得電腦科學的學士學位，同時，我已經在一間大型軟體公司工作了兩年。我有信心我的能力足以勝任這份工作。盼望能盡快有機會與您面談。

裘蒂‧凱恩

Dear Kane,

Glad to hear from you.

Your former experience was impressive. Could you please send us some of your previous works to let us know your ability better?

Regards,

Sammy Brown

親愛的凱恩：

很高興收到你的來信。

我們對你以往的經歷印象深刻。不知道你能否給我們看看你以前的作品，以便幫助我們更深入瞭解你的能力。

真誠地，

薩米・布朗

Dear Kane,

Thank you for paying attention to this job. We're very interested to get to know you better. Can we make an **appointment** this Tuesday afternoon?

Yours,

Sammy Brown

Chapter
1

Part 1

求職申請 Job applications

Part 2
Part 3
Part 4
Part 5
Part 6
Part 7

親愛的凱恩:

謝謝你關注這份工作。我們對你非常感興趣。能約在這週二下午見個面嗎?

真誠地,

薩米・布朗

重點單字記起來,寫信回信超精準

① **recruitment** n. 徵募、招募
The campus recruitment fair is going to be held next month. →校園徵才博覽會將在下個月舉行。

② **prestigious** adj. 有聲望的、享負名譽的
Surprisingly, the prestigious company went bankrupt yesterday. →令人驚訝的是,那間名聲極佳的公司昨天宣布破產了。

③ **competence** n. 能力、勝任、稱職
If you can't exhibit your competence for this position, we'll have to fire you.→如果你無法證明你能勝任這個職位,我們就只能開除你。

④ **convenience** n. 方便、合宜
Please reply at your earliest convenience.
→請儘早回覆。

⑤ **appointment** n. 任命、約定、任命的職位、會面
Have you forgotten that you have a very important appointment this afternoon?
→你是不是忘記今天下午你有個很重要的會議?

Unit 03 | 他人推薦信函

需要**幫他人寫推薦信**時，該怎麼寫呢？

To whom it may concern,

I am pleased to **recommend** Edward Young to you. I have known him for five years as his direct **supervisor**. He is an outstanding salesman who can always achieve his sales **objective** on time. In addition, his team work spirit and professional working attitude make him a star leader in our team. I have firm confidence in his **expertise** and I believe he would be a great staff in any company.

If you have any further query, please don't hesitate to contact me.

Yours truly,

Doris Silverstone

致敬啟者:

很榮幸地向您推薦愛德華‧楊。作為他的直屬主管，我已經認識他五年了。他是一個總能如期完成銷售目標的出色業務員。此外，他富有團隊合作的精神和專業的工作態度，使他輕易的成為我們團隊的王牌領導者。我對他的專業技能非常有信心，並相信他在任何一個公司都將會是一個非常能幹的員工。

如果您需要更多資訊，請隨時與我聯繫。

誠摯地，

多莉絲‧斯爾維斯通

Chapter
1

Part 1

求職申請 Job applications

Part 2
Part 3
Part 4
Part 5
Part 6
Part 7

收到**他人推薦信**時，該怎麼回呢？　　　— □ ✕

Ms./ Mrs. Silverstone,

Thank you for your recommendation. We're very interested in getting to know Mr. Young further. Could you please provide his detailed profile?

Best regards,

Tom Waits

HR Dept.

斯爾維斯通女士：

謝謝您的推薦信。我們公司對楊先生非常感興趣，想瞭解他更多的資訊。能否麻煩您提供他的詳細資料？

誠摯地祝福，

湯姆・維茨

人事部

不同的答覆還可以怎麼回呢？　　　— □ ✕

Dear Doris,

Your letter comes just right in the time; our company is in need of good salesmen.

But, pardon me for speaking frankly, why are you willing to part with such an outstanding staff? As your old partner and friend, tell me the truth won't bother you much, right?

Looking forward to your reply.

Best regards,

Tom Waits

親愛的桃莉絲：

你的信來得正是時候，我們公司正需要好的業務人員。

但恕我直言，你怎麼捨得這麼優秀的員工離開？作為你的老夥伴和老朋友，跟我說實話不難吧？

靜候回覆。

誠摯地祝福，

湯姆・維茨

 重點單字記起來，寫信回信超精準

① **recommend** ⓥ 建議、推薦、勸告、介紹
Can you recommend and introduce your signature dish? →你能向我們推薦並介紹你們的招牌料理嗎？

② **supervisor** ⓝ 監督人、管理人、指導者
Our supervisor is a very inspiring and encouraging person.
→我們的主管是個非常激勵人心且會鼓勵他人的人。

③ **objective** adj. 客觀的 ⓝ 目的、目標
Find your objective before you rush into anything.
→在草率做事之前，先找到你的目標。

④ **expertise** ⓝ 專業（技能）
You must show your expertise so as to win approval.
→你必須展現你的專業才能贏得認同。

Unit 04 | 請求安排面試

希望能**安排面試**時，該怎麼寫呢？   — □ ✕

Dear Recruitment Manager,

My name is Judy Lynn and I am replying your advertisement of an Administrative Assistant in Taiwan Daily. I have more than two years of experience in a local trading company and I have obtained a Bachelor degree in Administration Management. As you may read about my detail information in my CV, my **qualification** meets your requirements to the Administrative Assistant position. In order to have a face to face **communication** about this opportunity, I sincerely hope you may arrange an interview. I'm available from 9 a.m. to 6 p.m. during weekdays.

Looking forward to your early reply.

Yours truly,

Judy Lynn

親愛的招聘經理：

我叫裘蒂・林，我來信是想應徵貴公司在台灣日報上刊登的行政助理一職。我曾在一家本地貿易公司任職兩年多，並且我已經獲得了主修行政管理的學士學位。如您在我的履歷中讀到的詳細資訊，我的條件完全符合貴公司對此一職位的需求。為了得到面對面的交流機會，我真誠希望您能給我安排一次面試。我平日早上九點到晚上六點之間都有空。

殷切期待您的早日回覆！

裘蒂・林

Dear Judy,

I understand your status of mind, but what I'm going to say might **disappoint** you. As you can see from the Administration Assistant Wanted, our company won't accept people who have no experience working in foreign company.

Hope you can understand and wish you a bright future.

Sincerely yours,

Collin Handson

HR Manger

親愛的裘蒂：

我理解你的心情，但我接下來要說的可能會讓你失望：如您在我們的行政助理招聘啟事上能看到的，我們不接受沒有外商公司工作經歷的求職者。

希望你理解，並祝前程似錦。

人事經理，

科林・漢德森

Dear Judy,

We receive many resumes everyday and will go through all of them to pick up those qualified, and then go to the interview phase in late September.

It seems **unfair** to other candidates if we interview you now, right? I understand your status of mind, but please be patient.

Chapter
1

Part 1

求職申請 Job applications

Part 2
Part 3
Part 4
Part 5
Part 6
Part 7

Sincerely yours,

Collin Handson

HR Manger

親愛的裘蒂：

我們每天都會收到很多履歷，我們會仔細閱讀每一份，並篩選出合格者，於九月底進入面試階段。

如果我們現在就對你進行面試，對其他應徵者來說好像不大公平吧？我理解你的心情，但請保持耐心。

人事經理，

科林・漢德森

重點單字 記起來，寫信回信超精準

① **communication** n. 傳達、交流、交往、通信
Constant communications are important in a healthy relationship. →頻繁溝通在一段健康的關係中是很重要的。

② **qualification** n. 資格、條件
I'm sure my academic background meets the qualification for the position.
→我相信我的學術背景符合這個職位的條件。

③ **disappoint** v. 辜負⋯的期望、令人失望
The exhibition disappointed me to the point where I wanted to get a refund. →這場展覽令我失望到想要求退款。

④ **unfair** adj. 不公平的、不公正的
What he said to you was extremely unfair.
→他對你說的話極其不公。

Unit 05 | 詢問面試結果

想要**詢問面試**的結果時，該怎麼寫呢？ 　─ □ ✕

Dear Mr. Lucas,

It was really nice to meet you during our interview. As you previously **mentioned**, I should expect your feedback about the outcome of our meeting by May 15, 2020. Now, it has been past for two days, hence, I think maybe I should write to ask about it.I would appreciate a prompt reply.

I am sincerely expecting your feedback.

Yours faithfully,

Kate Moss

親愛的盧卡斯先生：

上次和您的面試很愉快。如您上次所提到的，我會於2020年5月15日之前得到您回覆的面試結果。現在時間已經過了兩天，我想也許我該寫信和您確認一下。如果您能儘快回覆，我將感激不盡。

殷切期盼您的回覆！

真誠地，

凱特・莫斯

Chapter
1

Part 1

求職申請 Job applications

Part 2
Part 3
Part 4
Part 5
Part 6
Part 7

回覆對方詢問面試的結果時，該怎麼回呢？ — □ ✕

Ms. Moss,

I have to apologize for the delay. Last week, our **server** broke down, so we were not able to make any phone calls. It will be fixed up within today and all the interviewees would receive our calls no less than tomorrow.

Sincerely yours,

Lucas Berlinman

莫斯女士：

抱歉出現這樣的延遲。我們公司的伺服器上週壞了，無法打電話通知各位。今天之內就會修好，所有面試者最晚明天就會接到電話。

真誠地，

盧卡斯‧博林曼

不同的答覆還可以怎麼回呢？ — □ ✕

Ms. Moss,

It's strange that you haven't received our mail. We sent it out 3 days ago. Please check the attached file to find the result. I'm sure you will **forgive** this little unpleasant delay after you see it.

Sincerely yours,

Lucas Berlinman

莫斯女士：

你沒收到我們在三天前就寄發出的郵件，真是太奇怪了。請查收附件中的面試結果。看到結果以後，相信你一定會忘記這小小的不愉快。

真誠地，

盧卡斯・博林曼

 重點單字 記起來，寫信回信超精準

① **mention** vt. 說起、提到、談到、提及、論及 n. 提及、說起
I remembered that you mentioned something about AI last time we met.
→我記得上次我們見面時你提到了有關人工智慧的事。

② **server** n. 伺服器
The server couldn't function, so all of you are required to work from home.
→伺服器無法運作，所以你們全部都必須在家工作。

③ **forgive** vt. 原諒
My life motto is to forgive and forget.
→我的人生座右銘就是原諒與忘記。

Unit 06 | 答謝公司錄取

收到**錄取通知**想到回信感謝時，該怎麼寫呢？ ▬ ☐ ✕

Dear Mr. Lucas,

Thank you for offering me the position as a sales assistant. It is my honor to be a member of your team and I am **excitedly** expecting to start work on 10 of June, 2020. I will work hard and try my best to learn and get familiar with our business soon.

Yours sincerely,

Kate Moss

尊敬的盧卡斯先生：

非常感謝您雇用我做為貴公司的銷售助理。能加入您的團隊讓我感到十分榮幸，並期待2020年6月10日到公司上班的那天儘早到來。我會努力工作，並盡最大努力學習及熟悉我們的業務。

真誠地，

凱特‧莫斯

回覆求職者的感謝信時，該怎麼回呢？　— □ ✕

Dear Kate,

You **deserve** this position and our warm welcome.Now, the whole department is looking forward to your joining us. I believe you will perform excellently to win everyone's attention. Just enjoy!

Cheers,

Lucas Berlinman

....

親愛的凱特：

你用實力得到了這個職位，也將得到我們的熱烈歡迎：現在整個部門都在期待著你加入我們。相信你能用出色的的表現吸引所有人的注意。好好享受吧！

真誠地，

盧卡斯・博林曼

不同的答覆還可以怎麼回呢？　— □ ✕

Dear Kate,

Welcome to our **marvelous** team! You'll soon find yourself falling in love with every member and you can go **nowhere** without them. We just can't wait to see you right away, so we decide to hold a welcome party this Saturday night, at Rock Stone Bar. Please let us know if you can join us!

Cheers,

Lucas Berlinman

Chapter
1

Part 1

求職申請 Job applications

Part 2
Part 3
Part 4
Part 5
Part 6
Part 7

親愛的凱特：

歡迎加入我們這個神奇的團隊！很快你就會愛上所有成員，不願和他們分開。我們等不及想馬上見到你，因此決定這週六晚在滾石酒吧舉行一個歡迎會。請讓我們知道你能否出席！

真誠地，

盧卡斯·博林曼

 重點單字記起來，寫信回信超精準

① **excitedly** adv. 興奮地、激動地
I waited excitedly for the graduation ceremony.
→我興奮地等待著畢業典禮的到來。

② **deserve** v. 值得、應得
You deserved the year-end bonus!
→年終獎金是你應得的！

③ **marvelous** adj. 驚人的、不可思議的
The acrobatic performance was simply marvelous.
→特技表演簡直驚奇。

④ **nowhere** n. 無處、任何地方、無名之地
I feel like I am stuck in the middle of nowhere.
→我覺得我被困在無人知曉之地。

Unit 07 | 婉拒錄取通知

收到錄取通知但是**想要婉拒**時，該怎麼寫呢？ ▬ ☐ ✕

Dear Mr. Lucas,

Thank you for the offer, but I am **terribly** sorry to tell you that I already accepted another job three days ago. I think that **position** suits me better. I hope you will find the right talent soon.

Thanks again for your appreciation.

Yours sincerely,

Kate Moss

親愛的盧卡斯先生：

感謝您錄取我，但是非常抱歉，我必須告訴您我已經在三天前已經接受了另一份工作。我覺得那份工作更適合我。祝您能儘快找到更合適的人選。

再次感謝您對我的賞識。

真誠地，

凱特・莫斯

Chapter

1

Part 1

求職申請 Job applications

Part 2
Part 3
Part 4
Part 5
Part 6
Part 7

收到錄取者的**婉拒信**時，該怎麼回呢？　　— □ ✕

Dear Kate,

Everybody has the right to **pursue** what he wants. I respect your choice; you don't have to feel sorry about this.

Hopefully, we can work together when there's another chance. Wish you a brighter future.

Lucas Berlinman

親愛的凱特：

每個人都有追求自己想要東西的權利。我尊重你的選擇，你不必為此感到抱歉。

希望日後有機會能共事。祝前程似錦。

盧卡斯・博林曼

不同的答覆還可以怎麼回呢？　　— □ ✕

Dear Kate,

It's a pity we can't work together. Your performance in the interview was really impressive. Hope we can **collaborate** in the future. Good luck!

Lucas Berlinman

親愛的凱特：

不能和你共事實在很遺憾。你在面試中的表現真的很令人印象深刻。希望我們能有機會在未來合作。祝好運！

盧卡斯・博林曼

重點單字記起來，寫信回信超精準

① **terribly** （口語）**adj.** 非常地
I'm terribly sorry for the trouble.
→造成麻煩我非常抱歉。

② **position** **n.** 位置、職位、狀態 **v.** 安置、決定⋯⋯ 的位置
You need to position the gear here to ensure proper functions of the machine.
→你需要把器材放在這裡以確保機器正常運作。

③ **pursue** **vt.** 從事、追趕、繼續、糾纏
I don't know what I want to pursue in life.
→我不知道我在人生中想要追求什麼。

④ **collaborate** **v.** 合作
The two companies collaborated in helping the government for the disease control.
→這兩間公司合作起來幫助政府防疫。

Note

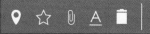

Unit 01 | 詢問產品資訊

要詢問**產品相關資料**時，該怎麼寫呢？

Dear Miss Zhang,

We learnt from the **advertisement** that your company produces electronic products of high quality. Since we found that they are in high demand in **local** market, we'd like to get more of them. Is it possible that you send details of your products, including sizes, prices, and also samples to us?

Looking forward to hearing from you!

Yours sincerely,

Lily Wang

親愛的張小姐：

我們從您的廣告中獲悉貴公司致力於生產高品質的電子產品。由於我們發現貴公司的電子產品在當地市場有龐大需求，因此我們打算買進更多的相關產品。不知您是否可以寄一份貴公司產品的細節，包含尺寸、價格，以及樣品給我們呢？

期待您的回信！

真誠地，

王莉莉

Chapter

1

Part 1

Part 2

處理訂單 Processing orders

Part 3
Part 4
Part 5
Part 6
Part 7

收到**產品受到關注**的信時，該怎麼回呢？ — □ ✕

Dear Miss Wang,

We welcome your enquiry on 9th of July and thank you for your interest in our products. We enclose our **illustrated catalogue** with the details you asked for. Samples of our products about which you inquired in the latest email are being sent to you today. If our products and prices meet your requirements, we will be very glad to start a business relationship with you. Thank you for your support to our company.

We are looking forward to your first order.

Yours faithfully,

Alex Zhang

....

親愛的王莉莉女士：

很高興收到您7月9日的來信，也非常感謝您關注我們的產品。隨信附上我們的產品目錄及其他您詢問的詳細資訊，根據您上一封郵件中的要求，樣品也今天也會送達到您手中。如果我們的產品及價格符合您的要求，我們將非常高興與您建立商務關係。感謝您對本公司的支持！

期待您的第一筆訂單。

真誠地，

艾力克斯張

不同的答覆還可以怎麼回呢？ — □ ✕

Dear Miss Wang,

We have received your enquiry on 18th of April with thanks and are glad that you are interested in our products. Enclosed are a copy of our latest catalogue and a price-list of our products. Our products are all superior in quality and have been sold to many countries and regions in Europe, America, and Africa. We are confident that you will be satisfied with the goods excellent in quality and reasonable in price.

If you need further information apart from the above-mentioned catalogue and price list, please don't hesitate to let us know.

We are looking forward to doing business with you in the near future.

Yours sincerely,

Alex Zhang

親愛的張小姐：

感謝您4月18號的來信諮詢，也很高興您對我們的產品感興趣。附件是我們最新的產品目錄和報價單。我們的產品品質一流，暢銷歐美、非洲等多個國家和地區。相信我們物美價廉的產品一定會讓您滿意。

如果除了上面的資料您還需要其他產品資訊，敬請來信諮詢。

期待很快就能與您合作。

真誠地，

張艾力克斯

 重點單字記起來，寫信回信超精準

① **advertisement** n. 廣告、宣傳
This advertisement aims to promote the idea of work-life balance. →此廣告只在倡導工作與生活的平衡。

② **local** n. 局部、當地居民 adj. 當地的、局部的、地方性的
My parents show their support and mainly buy local produce. →我爸媽展現支持，主要都買當地農產品。

③ **illustrate** v. 說明、插圖於（書籍）
This five-year-old girl illustrated what she saw with drawing. →這位五歲的小女孩用繪畫說明所見的事物。

④ **catalogue** n. 目錄 v. 編入目錄
The department store sent the catalogue of the products at special price. →百貨公司寄來特價品的目錄。

Unit 02 | 樣品寄出通知

想要通知對方**樣品已寄出**時，該怎麼寫呢？ ▬ ⊡ ✕

Dear Mr. Flower,

I'd like to inform you that the samples you **requested** were shipped today by UPS Express. I have attached a price and color list in this e-mail, too. Please **notify** me **immediately** when they arrive. Thanks a lot!

I am looking forward to your response.

Sincerely yours,

BU Company

親愛的弗洛爾先生：

特此通知您，您訂購的樣品已經在今天由UPS快遞寄出。隨信附上了價格表和顏色表。收到貨物時請馬上通知我，感激不盡！

期待您的回應。

真誠地，

BU 公司敬上

BU Company,

Thank you for the **rapid** shipment. I will pay attention to its arrival time. I will call you once receiving it.

Sincerely yours,

Flower

BU公司：

謝謝你們這麼快就寄來了。我會注意查收。一收到馬上打電話給你們。

真誠地，

弗洛爾

BU Company,

Sorry, I forget to inform you that I've already received your sample 2 hours ago. Hope this won't be a problem.

Sincerely yours,

Flower

BU公司：

不好意思忘了通知你們，2小時前我已收到你們的快遞。希望沒耽誤你們。

真誠地，

弗洛爾

Chapter

1

Part 1

Part 2

處理訂單 Processing orders

Part 3
Part 4
Part 5
Part 6
Part 7

 重點單字記起來，寫信回信超精準

① **request** v. / n. 請求、需要
The table of content of the book was revised at your request. →此書的目錄已因應你的要求做修改。

② **immediately** adv. 直接地、立即、立刻
The government responded immediately after the first case of the disease.
→在第一例出現後，政府立即採取行動。

③ **notify** v. 通知
The fire alarm aims to notify everyone that there's a fire. →火警警報器的作用就是通知每個人有火災發生。

④ **rapid** adj. 迅速的
The situation of COVID-19 gets worse at a rapid speed in the world.
→新冠肺炎的疫情正迅速在世界各地擴散中。

Unit 03 | 要求回報進度

需要對方**隨時回報**商品進度時，該怎麼寫呢？　

Dear Sir or Madam,

We have studied your catalogue and price list. After a conference in our company, we chose you to be our future business partner. Enclosed please find our order No. CN037.

We have decided to buy a large quantity of high-quality women shoes from you and we would like to **stress** that from now on, please notify us the latest information on our ordered goods. Timely **feedback** will be **beneficial** to us in the near future.

Thank you in advance for your cooperation.

Yours Sincerely,

Lily

親愛的先生／女士：

我已看過貴公司的產品目錄和價格清單。本公司經過開會討論決定與您公司結為貿易夥伴。附件中是本公司的訂貨單No.CN037。

我們已經決定從貴公司購買大量的優質女鞋。我們想強調的是從今以後請及時通知我們關於本公司訂購的貨物情況。及時的資訊回饋將使我們雙方受益。

預先感謝貴公司的配合。

真誠地，

莉莉

Chapter
1

Part 1
Part 2
Part 3
Part 4
Part 5
Part 6
Part 7

處理訂單 Processing orders

收到對方**叮囑回報**進度時，該怎麼回呢？ — □ ✕

Dear Lily,

We are pleased to confirm your letter of 7th of Nov. with an order No. CN037.

Thank you for your decision to choose our products and we are confident that the sales will satisfy you. For this request, we will inform you the latest condition of your products.

We look forward to the continued business.

Yours faithfully,

Charles

親愛的莉莉：

很高興收到你的來信，並受到貴公司的訂購單No.Cn037。謝謝貴公司決定訂購我們的產品。我們也有信心我們產品的良好銷售量必定讓貴公司滿意。對於你的要求，我們一定將貴公司訂購產品的最新進展即時告知。

期待與您繼續合作。

真誠地，

查爾斯

不同的答覆還可以怎麼回呢？ — □ ✕

Dear Lily,

Thank you very much for your e-mail on 7th of Nov. and your order No. CN037. But we regret to inform you that the extreme weather has **hindered** our raw materials transportation, so we have to delay our manufacture. But we will notify you the moment when we begin the manufacturing process and let you know the information of your goods in the following days.

Yours faithfully,

Charles

親愛的莉莉：

謝謝您十一月七日的來信，並附上貴公司的訂購單No.Cn037。但是很遺憾的，必須告訴您由於極端天氣阻擾了本公司的原物料運輸，所以我們不得不延誤生產時程。但是我們將會在開工時，第一時間告知您，也將在今後隨時提供您訂購產品的資訊。

真誠地，

查爾斯

 重點單字記起來，寫信回信超精準

① **stress** n. 壓力 v. 強調
Nowadays, even elementary school students have stress from schoolwork. →現今，即使國小生都有課業壓力。

② **feedback** n. 回饋意見
Can you give them some feedback on the new advertisement? →你能給他們一些關於新廣告的意見嗎？

③ **beneficial** adj. 有益的
Probiotics is considered beneficial to our health.
→我們認為益生菌對健康有好處。

④ **hinder** v. 妨礙
Financial problem hinders me from buying a new car.
→經濟問題使我無法我買新車。

Unit 04 | 詢問庫存資料

想要**詢問產品庫存**時，該怎麼寫呢？　　─ □ ✕

Dear Mr. Burns,

Your product, camera DSC-T700, is sold well here with its high quality and **favorable** price. Therefore, we decide to purchase more of them. Please check out your **inventory** to see if you have two hundred more for another delivery.

Looking forward to receiving an early reply.

Yours sincerely,

Jack Jones

親愛的伯恩斯先生：

鑒於貴公司型號為 DSC-T700 的相機品質優良、價格優惠且銷量佳，我們決定再追加訂購數量。煩請確認該型號是否還有庫存，我們需要再追加二百台。

殷切期待您的回覆！

真誠地，

傑克・瓊斯

Dear Jones,

Congratulations for your good sales!

We still have more products in our inventory. We are going to deliver the 200 cameras your company needed recently. For some extra need, please contact with us any time.

We thank you again for the above order.

Yours sincerely,

Burns

親愛的瓊斯：

恭喜您取得良好的銷售業績！

本公司生產的DSC-T700相機目前還有庫存，貴公司所需要追加的200台相機，本公司將於近日出貨。如有其他需求，請隨時與我們聯繫。

再次感謝您的訂購。

真誠地，

伯恩斯

Dear Jones,

DSC-T700 has gotten **outstanding** achievement in oversea market, so we have no **stock** temporarily. The next batch of the camera will be produced till month. If you have any need then, please send us your order at your earliest convenience. We can also consider providing you a discount for large quantity.

Looking forward to the next cooperation. Best wishes.

Chapter
1

Part 1

Part 2

處理訂單 Processing orders

Part 3
Part 4
Part 5
Part 6
Part 7

Yours faithfully,

Burns

....

親愛的瓊斯：

由於本公司生產的DSC-T700相機在海外市場銷量很好，所以目前本公司已經沒有庫存，下一批相機將於下個月出廠，如果屆時貴公司還有需要，請及早通知我們。如果您大批量訂購，我們會考慮提供折扣。

期待下次合作。祝福您 。

真誠地，

伯恩斯

 重點單字記起來，寫信回信超精準

① **favorable** adj. 有利的、良好的、贊成的、討人喜歡的
The Board is favorable to the project.
→董事會贊成此專案。

② **inventory** n. 存貨（清單）
Are there still any inventories of this new product?
→還有這項新產品的存貨嗎？

③ **outstanding** adj. 傑出的
Andy had outstanding performance in the relay race.
→Andy 在接力賽中有傑出的表現

④ **stock** n. 存貨、股票
Currently, we don't have enough stock in the shop.
→目前我們店裡的存貨不夠。

Unit 05 | 詳細交貨日期

想要詢問**交貨日期**時，該怎麼寫呢？　　— □ ✕

Dear Mr. Brown,

We wish to draw your attention to our order on 20 of May (Order No. 728) for car **components**. Would you please inform us how long it will take to make delivery of this order? Couldn't you ship the goods before early June? **Moreover**, please mail the invoice of this order to our company.

We thank you in advance for your cooperation.

Truly yours,

Henry Davis

親愛的布朗先生：

麻煩您查一下敝公司於5月20日訂購的（訂單編號：728）汽車零部件的訂單，敬請告知什麼時候能出貨。能否保證於六月初之前到貨。此外，請將發票寄送到本公司。

感謝您的合作！

真誠地，

亨利・大衛斯

Chapter

1

Part 1

Part 2

處理訂單 Processing orders

Part 3
Part 4
Part 5
Part 6
Part 7

收到詢問**交貨日期**的信時，該怎麼回呢？   – □ ✕

Dear Mr. Davis,

I have checked your order on 20 of May (Order No.728) for car components. These goods have already proceeded to the shipment process at the end of May and it's expected to arrive at early of June. The **invoice** was attached along with goods.

I am look forward to cooperating with you again. Thank you.

Yours sincerely,

Brown

....

親愛的大衛斯：

貴公司於5月20日所訂購的汽車零部件，本公司已於5月底進入運送程序，預計6月初到貨，發票已連同貨物一起寄送到貴公司。

期待與貴公司再次合作。謝謝您。

真誠地，

布朗

不同的答覆還可以怎麼回呢？   – □ ✕

Dear Mr. Davis,

I'm terribly sorry that we have to make you disappointed this time. As you know, because of our insistence on high-quality products, car components produced in our company are in high demand for the past few months. So, it may not be possible to deliver goods for any customer ahead of time. I hope you can understand. In accordance with the **provisions** of the contract, we will ship these goods you ordered on 28th of May and the invoice will also send to your company with the goods.

We thank you for your full cooperation.

Yours truly,

Brown

親愛的大衛斯：

非常抱歉這次可能得讓您失望了。由於本公司產品品質上乘，幾個月來我們生產的汽車零件都供不應求。所以我們沒有多餘的庫存為任何顧客提前出貨，希望您能諒解。貴公司於5月20日所訂購的汽車零件，本公司將於5月28日按照合約規定準時出貨，屆時，發票將和貨物一起送到貴公司。

謝謝合作！

真誠地，

布朗

重點單字 記起來，寫信回信超精準

① **component** n. 部件、組件、成份
We'll have to delay the shipment for the shortage of some components. →因部分零件缺貨，我們必須延遲出貨時間。

② **moreover** adv. 而且、此外
Moreover, the rain continued for an entire month.
→此外，雨下了整整一個月。

③ **invoice** n. 發票、出貨單 v. 開發票
I'll invoice you for the No. 567 order.
→我會開立訂單編號567的發票給您。

④ **provisions** n. 條款
This statute contains interim provisions that we should all abide by. →此法令包含我們都應遵守的暫時條款。

Unit 06 | 商品價格運費

想要**詢問商品的價格和運費**時，該怎麼寫呢？ — □ ✕

Dear Mr. Willy,

We are very interested in your newly-produced **laser** printer which has been exhibited last month. The purpose of this letter is to inquire about the price of this product, also the **freight** and handling **fees**.

Please let us know on what **terms** you can give us some discount.

Your early offer will be highly appreciated.

Yours sincerely,

Topher Grass

親愛的威利先生：

我們對貴公司上個月展出的新雷射印表機很感興趣，因此希望您能就這款新機型提供我們一個最新報價（包含運費和手續費）。

敬請告知我們什麼條件下才能享有折扣。

請早日報價，感激不盡。

真誠地，

托弗·葛拉斯

Dear Mr. Grass,

The quotation for our newly-produced laser printer including the freight and procedure fee is enclosed in this letter, and you can earn 2% discount if the quantity of the laser printer that you buy is more than 50.

Looking forward to doing business with you.

Yours sincerely,

Willy

親愛的格拉斯：

關於本公司新進生產的雷射印表機的運費和手續費價格，請參見附件。至於本公司享有折扣的條件是，如果您購買雷射印表機的數量超過50台就可以享受2%的折扣。

期待能與貴公司合作。

真誠地，

威利

Dear Mr. Grass,

Thank you for your interest in our new product. The price of the newly-produced laser printer, the freight, and the procedure fees are still under discussion. As soon as the result comes out, we will inform you at the first time. In addition, because the laser printer is a new product, we don't have any discount. Hope you can understand.

Best regards.

Willy

Chapter
1

Part 1

Part 2

處理訂單 Processing orders

Part 3
Part 4
Part 5
Part 6
Part 7

親愛的格拉斯：

感謝您對我們新產品的關注。本公司新進生產的雷射印表機的運費和手續費價格還在討論中,等到結果一出來,我們會第一時間跟您聯繫。另外,由於該雷射印表機是新產品,所以我們暫時不會提供任何折扣。希望您能諒解。

真誠地,

威利

 重點單字記起來,寫信回信超精準

① **laser** n. 雷射
The laser beam fixed his eyesight painlessly.
→雷射光束使他的視力無痛的恢復了正常。

② **freight** v. 運送、裝貨 n. 貨物、運費、船貨
This order will be sent to you by freight.
→這批訂單將以貨運寄送給您。

③ **fee** n. 費用、酬金、小費
The handling fee is rather high in this bank.
→這間銀行的手續費相當高。

④ **term** n. 術語、學期、期限、條款
The terms in this contract are all made according to our negotiation.
→這份合約中的條款皆根據我們的協商訂立。

Unit 07 | 確認產品價格

遇到**標價和實收價不符合**的情況時，該怎麼寫呢？

Dear Mr. Jason,

Yesterday, I bought a pair of **soccer** boots of your brand. The price tag says 1000 U.S. dollars, but I found out that they charged me 1,200 dollars. I didn't know the reason.

I write this e-mail to you with the hope that you can provide me a reasonable explanation. I am your **regular** customer and I don't want this issue affect my trust in your company.

Yours sincerely,

Collins

親愛的傑森先生：

昨天我在貴公司買了一雙足球鞋，標價1000元，可是結帳時卻被收了1200元，我不知道是什麼原因。

我寫這封郵件給您是希望您能為我做出合理的解釋。我是貴公司的常客，我不希望這件事影響我對貴公司的信任度。

真誠地，

科林斯

Chapter

1

Part 1

Part 2

處理訂單 Processing orders

Part 3

Part 4

Part 5

Part 6

Part 7

收到**確認商品價格**的信時，該怎麼回呢？　─ □ ✕

Dear Mr. Collins,

I'm sorry to make you upset. Because of the negligence of our staff, the marked price of that soccer boots is wrong.

If you like, we will refund 200 U.S. dollars to you in **compensation** for your emotional **distress**. We thank you for drawing our attention to a situation of which we had been quite unaware before. Please accept our apologies for the inconvenience you have been caused.

Yours sincerely,

Jason

親愛的科林斯先生：

很抱歉由於我們的疏忽使您不悦。由於職員的疏忽，您買的這雙足球鞋的標價錯了。

如果您願意，我們會退還給您200美元，作為對您的精神賠償。感謝您為我們指出服務差強人意之處。對您造成不便我們深感抱歉。

真誠地，

傑森

不同的答覆還可以怎麼回呢？　─ □ ✕

Dear Mr. Collins,

We thank you for your letter on 19 of August.

We are sorry to hear that we didn't provide a satisfactory service for you. The correct price of that pair of shoes should be 1200 U.S. dollars, but our staff made a mistake when they marked the price. You can return the product whenever it is convenient to you.

Apologize again for causing you trouble.

Yours sincerely,

Jason

親愛的科林斯先生：

感謝您8月19號的來信。

很抱歉先前我們並未提供令您滿意的服務，這雙鞋正確的標價的確是1200美元，但是我們的員工在標價時弄錯了。您隨時可以回來退貨。

再次為替您造成困擾而道歉。

真誠地，

傑森

 重點單字記起來，寫信回信超精準

① **soccer** n. 英式足球、足球
Would you like to join our soccer team?
→你想要加入我們的足球隊嗎？

② **regular** a. 規則的、規律的、固定的
I'm a regular customer here and I wonder if I can get a discount. →我是這裡的常客，我在想不能有點優惠。

③ **compensation** n. 補償
We filed for lawsuit for financial compensation.
→我們訴諸法律以求金錢補償。

④ **distress** n. 悲痛 v. 使悲痛
Maria was in distress over the loss of her husband.
→失去丈夫使瑪莉亞悲痛。

Unit 08 | 產品送達日期

遇到**產品送達日期**有誤時，該怎麼寫呢？ ー口✕

Dear Jack,

I would like to inquire about the specific arrival date of the goods we ordered on 13 of February, which were **originally** scheduled to arrive on the 12th of this month, but I have not received the goods till today. Did I make a mistake of the date? Or something happened in delivery? Please give me reply as soon as possible.

Yours,

Mary

親愛的傑克：

我想請教一下，本公司2月13日訂購產品確切的到貨日期。原定於本月12日到貨，可是我到現在都還沒有收到商品。是我記錯了，還是公司出貨出現了問題？請儘快給我回覆。

真誠地，

瑪麗

Dear Mary,

Upon inquiry, the goods have been issued. It may be the **logistics** problems. We will **coordinate** it soon and inform you of the exact arrival date.

We shall contact our agents and the port authorities to prevent delays occurring in this way in the future.

Yours,

Jack

親愛的瑪麗：

經查詢後，商品已經寄出。可能是物流出現問題，我們會儘快協調，給您答覆。

我們會與我們的代理商和港口相關部門取得聯繫，防止日後再次產生類似的情況。

真誠地，

傑克

Dear Mary:

We received your letter on 14 of March that concerned the delay of the goods of Order No. 221. I am terribly sorry. Due to the heavy **workload** recently, the delivery date was delayed for two days.

We shall do everything we can to ensure that similar mistakes do not happen again. Please accept our sincere apologies.

Chapter
1

Part 1
Part 2

處理訂單　Processing orders

Part 3
Part 4
Part 5
Part 6
Part 7

Yours,

Jack

親愛的瑪麗：

我們收到了您3月14日的來信向我們反映編號221的貨物送達延遲的問題。實在很抱歉，由於公司最近業務繁忙，所以出貨日期延遲了兩天。

我們保證日後一定不會讓類似的情況再次發生，在此致上我們的歉意。

真誠地，

傑克

重點單字 記起來，寫信回信超精準

① **originally** adv. 最初、起初、本來
Originally, we plan to go outing this weekend.
→原本我們計劃週末去遠足。

② **logistics** n. 物流
After investigation, we found out that the mistake was made in the logistics part.
→經過調查，我們發現出錯的部分是物流。

③ **coordinate** v. 協調、使一致
We need someone to coordinate the whole event.
→我們需要有人協調整個活動。

④ **workload** n. 工作量
My brother always complain about his heavy workloads.
→我弟弟總是抱怨他的工作量很重。

Unit 09 | 合約詳細內容

想要詳談**合約細節**時，該怎麼寫呢？ — □ ✕

Dear Ms. Zhang,

I'm pleased to contract a **canteen** business relationship with your company. We will do our best to provide all employees of your company a good service. However, the details on the food **retail** area is not specified in the contract, so I hope to discuss this issue with you again.

Yours sincerely,

Wang Hao

親愛的張小姐：

很高興能夠承包經營貴公司的員工餐廳業務。我們將竭誠為您公司全體員工提供良好的服務。不過，關於食品零售範圍明細，合約契約中沒有談及，因此希望能夠和您再次進行洽談。

真誠地，

王浩

Chapter

1

Part 1

Part 2

處理訂單 Processing orders

Part 3

Part 4

Part 5

Part 6

Part 7

收到**詢問合約細節**的信時，該怎麼回呢？　— □ ✕

Dear Mr. Wang,

We have received your letter concerning the details on the food retail area. We will reply to you as soon as possible after our internal discussions. Also, we want to know your opinion about the business **scope** of food retail. Given goodwill on both sides, I'm sure we can reach agreement.

Yours,

Zhang Dan

親愛的王先生：

我們已經收到你們關於討論食品零售範圍的信件，我們在內部討論後會儘快回覆您。同時，我們也需要瞭解一下您對食品零售範圍的看法。我相信在雙方都有誠意的基礎上我們一定能達成共識。

真誠地，

張丹

不同的答覆還可以怎麼回呢？　— □ ✕

Dear Mr. Wang,

We have reported the issue to the logistics **sector** and they haven't give us a result yet. We will send details to you at the first time when we get any information.

Yours,

Zhang Dan

親愛的王浩：

關於您提出的問題我們已經呈報給物流部門，具體細節正在商確中。我們將在得知結果後於第一時間通知您。

真誠地，

張丹

 重點單字記起來，寫信回信超精準

① **canteen** n. （工廠、學校等的）餐廳，販賣部
After being dismissed from the class, students usually go to canteen to buy some snacks.
→下課之後，學生經常去販賣部買零食。

② **retail** n. 零售 adj. 零售的 adv. 以零售方式；以零售價格 v. 零售
The retail price of the clothes is 50 dollars.
→這件衣服的零售價是五十元。

③ **scope** n. 範圍，領域
The scope of his doctoral dissertation is beyond our comprehension. →他的博士論文領域我們已經無法理解。

④ **sector** n. 部門、扇形
This is a private sector of the corporation and only VIPs have access to it.
→這是企業的私人部門，只有貴賓能進去。

Unit 10 | 退換產品時程

想要**確認產品退換**的時間時，該怎麼寫呢？ ─ ▢ ✕

Dear Bob,

Last week I found a **crack** on the newly-purchased cabinet bought from your shop. The staff has **identified** it as the quality problem of the **commodity** itself. So, I write this letter to see when it's convenient for me to go to your company and to **tackle** this problem.

Please give me reply as soon as possible.

Yours,

Tom

親愛的鮑勃：

上週我發現在貴公司購買的櫥櫃出現了裂痕，經工作人員鑒定確認是商品本身品質問題。寫這封信是想詢問，我什麼時候到貴公司處理比較方便？

請儘速回覆我。

真誠地，

湯姆

Dear Tom,

Your letter of May 29 regarding cabinet's quality problem came as a surprise, as the quality of our furniture has never let any customer down before. We feel deeply sorry for the inconvenience. You can come to our company anytime during the working hours.

I do hope this undesirable incident will not stand in the way of our future business.

Yours,

Bob

親愛的湯姆：

您5月29日反映櫥櫃品質問題的來信著實讓我們吃了一驚，因為我們的產品長期以來從未出過問題。很抱歉給您造成了困擾，您可以在任何有營業的時段前往本公司。

我非常希望這件不愉快的事件不會影響我們日後的合作。

真誠地，

鮑勃

不同的答覆還可以怎麼回呢？ — □ ✕

Dear Tom,

Sorry to make you upset. We are open every day of the week, all year. So, you can come any time you like. It's recommended that you avoid the peak of the weekend and come over here on weekdays.

Faithfully yours,

Tom

Chapter
1

Part 1

Part 2

處理訂單 Processing orders

Part 3
Part 4
Part 5
Part 6
Part 7

親愛的湯姆：

很抱歉造成您的不便，本公司全年無休，您任何一天都可以來公司調換。建議您避開週末高峰期，選擇週一至週五到公司調換。

真誠地，

鮑勃

 重點單字記起來，寫信回信超精準

① **crack** v 使破裂、爆裂 n 裂縫、爆裂聲
My grandfather cracked a nut and savor it.
→我爺爺敲開堅果品嚐其滋味。

② **identify** v 確認；識別；鑑定、（與……）認同；一致
I cannot identify his identity. →我辨認不出他的身分。

③ **commodity** n 商品、貨物、日用品
Fruit is an important commodity in Taiwan.
→水果是台灣重要的出口產品。

④ **tackle** v 著手對付（或處理）；與……交涉
Mr. White tackled the difficult problem, but he couldn't solve it. →懷特先生處理了這個難題，但未能解決。

Unit 11 | 產品配送費用

Dear Miss Zhang,

I am interested in some goods I saw online, so I would like to purchase them. I want to know how much EMS and **express** cost if they were sent to Taipei and how long the shipment will take.

Look forward to your reply!

Yours sincerely,

Wang May

親愛的張小姐：

我對於一些我在網路上看到的商品很感興趣，十分想購買它們。我想瞭解一下如果郵寄到台北，EMS及快遞各需多少錢，並且需要多久時間？

十分期待您的回覆！

真誠地，

王梅

Chapter
1

Part 1
Part 2

處理訂單　Processing orders

Part 3
Part 4
Part 5
Part 6
Part 7

收到詢問**產品配送**費用的信時，該怎麼回呢？ — □ ✕

Dear Miss Wang,

Thank you for your attention to our products and it's been a pleasure serving you. Express costs 12 yuan and EMS costs 18 yuan. Because our **brick-and-mortar** shop is located in Taipei, you will receive the goods on the day or the next day of the **confirmation** of your order.

Thank you for your support to our on-line shop!

Yours sincerely,

Alice Zhang

親愛的王小姐：

非常感謝您對本店產品的關注，十分榮幸能為您服務。如果您選擇快遞需要12.0元，EMS18.0元。因為產品的店面就在台北，在您下單的當天或隔天就能收到商品。

感謝您對我們網路商店的支持！

真誠地，

愛麗絲張

不同的答覆還可以怎麼回呢？ — □ ✕

Dear Miss Wang,

Thank you for your attention to our products and I will serve you sincerely. I am very sorry that your product is **temporarily** out of stock and the new batch of products will only be shipped two weeks later. I apologize for it.

Yours sincerely,

Alice Zhang

親愛的王小姐：

非常感謝您對本店產品的關注，我一定竭誠為您服務。但是非常遺憾，您所訂購的產品暫時缺貨，大概兩週後才會有新的一批產品運到。我很抱歉。

真誠地，

愛麗絲張

 重點單字記起來，寫信回信超精準

① **express** [v.] 表達、快遞 [n.] 快遞、快車
I don't know how to express my emotions in words.
→我不知道如何透過語言表達我的情緒。

② **brick-and-mortar**
[adj.] 實際存在的，實體的 [n.] 實體；實體店
People now seldom buy books in the brick-and-mortar bookstores. →人們現在很少在實體書店買書。

③ **confirmation** [n.] 確定；確認；批准
You will receive email confirmation after booking hotels with our app.
→在使用我們的應用程式訂房後，您將會收到電子郵件確認信。

④ **temporarily** [adv.] 暫時地，臨時地
The arena is temporarily closed due to COVID-19.
→因應新型冠狀肺炎疫情，這個活動場所現在暫時關閉。

Unit 12 | 商品進行出貨

要寄出**商品出貨通知**時，該怎麼寫呢？

Dear Mr. Murphy,

This is a shipment notice. We have shipped your order NO. 0855 on 21 of April, 2020. And I also sent you the relevant shipping **documents** by fax. Please check.

You should receive the goods you ordered by 28 of May, 2020 if there is no **accident**.

Please let us know when they arrive. Thanks very much!

Yours truly,

LD Company

親愛的墨菲先生：

這是一封出貨通知。您訂單編號為0855的產品已於2020年4月21日出貨。相關資訊也已經傳真給您，請查收。沒有意外的話，您將在2020 年5月28日收到商品。

到貨時請通知我們。謝謝！

真誠地，

LD 公司

收到對方的**出貨通知**時，該怎麼回呢？　　　− □ ×

LD Company,

Sorry to bother but I found out that my address was **mistakenly** filled in while I placed the order. Is there anything I can do to make things back to the right way?

Regards,

Evonne Chan

LD公司：

非常抱歉，我發現我下單時寫錯地址了。現在有什麼辦法能補救嗎？

真誠地，

陳伊馮

不同的答覆還可以怎麼回呢？　　　− □ ×

LD Company,

I'll be on a business trip from tomorrow, so I can't **sign** for your goods. Could you please change the arrival date? Many thanks.

Regards,

Evonne Chan

LD公司：

我將從明天開始出差，恐怕沒辦法簽收貨品。能換個日期送來嗎？謝謝。

真誠地，

陳伊馮

Chapter
1
Part 1
Part 2
處理訂單 Processing orders
Part 3
Part 4
Part 5
Part 6
Part 7

重點單字記起來，寫信回信超精準

① **document** n. 文件、公文、文檔、證件 v. 用文件證明
Please back up this document in case of any emergencies.
→請將文件備份以防緊急需要。

② **accident** n. 事故、機遇、意外事件、意外
The accident caused severe casualties.
→這場意外傷亡慘重。

③ **mistakenly** adv. 錯誤地；被誤解地
He mistakenly took the wrong backpack.
→他誤拿了錯的背包。

④ **sign** v. 簽名、簽署
Please sign your name here.
→請在這裡簽名。

Unit 13 | 開放訂購產品

要通知開放**產品訂購**時，該怎麼寫呢？

Dear members,

First of all, we wish everyone a Merry Christmas in advance!

We are happy to inform you that you could come to buy any commodities as usual during holidays. Besides, you could choose whatever you like on the website of our mall, and we will provide the service of **cash on delivery**.

Please enjoy your shopping!

Sincerely yours,

Pacific Digital Products Mall

敬愛的會員們：

首先，預祝大家聖誕節快樂！

很高興通知大家，在假日期間，您依然可以正常購買商品。並且，您可以在商場的網頁上選擇您需要的商品，我們就會提供貨到付款服務。

祝您購物愉快！

真誠地，

太平洋數位購物中心

Chapter
1

Part 1

Part 2

處理訂單　Processing orders

Part 3
Part 4
Part 5
Part 6
Part 7

收到產品**開放訂購的通知**時，該怎麼回呢？ — □ ✕

Pacific Digital,

I placed an order 2 days ago, but there's no **response** up to now. Could you please help checking this?

Regards,

Sally Chou

太平洋數位：

我兩天前在你們網站上下了訂單，然後就石沉大海，至今沒有消息。能幫我查詢一下嗎？

真誠地，

周莎莉

不同的答覆還可以怎麼回呢？ — □ ✕

Pacific Digital,

It's **brilliant** of you to choose this way to **expand** your business and create a convenient life for people. I'll go to your website to have a look. Hope there's something I'm interested.

Regards,

Sally Chou

太平洋數位：

你們透過這種方式來擴張事業版圖真是太聰明了，而且這樣對大眾也更加便利。我會去網站上逛逛看有沒有自己喜歡的東西。

真誠地，

周莎莉

 重點單字記起來，寫信回信超精準

① **cash on delivery** ph. 貨到付款
It's very common to use cash on delivery when shopping online. →網路購物很常使用貨到付款。

② **response** n. 回答；答覆；反應
Our company hasn't received the response from the potential client. →我們公司還未收到潛在客戶的回覆。

③ **brilliant** adj. 光輝的；明亮的；出色的
He just came up with a brilliant idea.
→他剛想到一個出色的點子。

④ **expand** v. 擴張、膨脹
The balloon continued to expand and finally exploded in the sky. →氣球不斷膨脹，最後在空中爆炸了。

Unit 14 | 訂購產品缺貨

要告訴對方**產品缺貨**時，該怎麼寫呢？

Dear subscribers,

Because of the **unexpected** expanding sales during Christmas, we are so sorry to inform you that the new type of SUNSHINE computer you ordered has been out of stock.

However, we will restock at once. If you still wish to order it a week later, please let us know if you would like to have it **delivered** by express or you come to the mall to pick it up by yourself.

We are looking forward to **hearing from** you soon.

Sincerely yours,

Pacific Digital Products Mall

親愛的訂購客戶：

因為沒有預料到聖誕節的銷售量會劇增，我們很遺憾的在此通知您，您訂購的陽光新款電腦已經缺貨了。

不過我們很快就會進貨。如果一週後您還想要訂購，那麼請告知我們出貨方式，可以選擇快遞或是本人親自取貨。

期待您的回信。

真誠地，

太平洋數位購物中心

Pacific Digital,

Due to the fact that I'm **desperately** in need of the computer, I cannot wait until next week. I'll buy it somewhere else. Sure you'll understand.

Yours,

Arthur Hans

太平洋數位：

由於我非常想馬上擁有那台電腦，我等不到下週。我會去別的地方購買。你們一定能理解。

真誠地，

亞瑟・漢斯

Pacific Digital,

Thanks for your notification.

I'll go to your place to pick it up myself. Please kindly call me when the computer arrives.

Regards,

Arthur Hans

太平洋數位：

謝謝你們的通知。

我會去你們店裡親自取貨。電腦到了請打電話給我。

真誠地，

亞瑟・漢斯

Chapter

1

Part 1

Part 2

處理訂單 Processing orders

Part 3

Part 4

Part 5

Part 6

Part 7

 重點單字記起來，寫信回信超精準

① **unexpected** adj. 想不到的；意外的；突如其來的
My aunt paid me an unexpected visit.
→我阿姨出乎意料地前來看我。

② **deliver** v. 發表、遞送
She delivered an amazing speech at the annual convention. →她在年度會議上發表了一場精彩演說。

③ **hear from** ph. 從……得到消息（信）
I haven't heard from him since he left.
→他離開後我就沒再聽過他的消息了。

④ **desperately** adv. 拼命地、絕望地、極度地
The man desperately tried to reach the floating wood.
→男子拼命地試圖抓住浮木。

Unit 15 | 確認產品付款

要告訴**對方已付款**時，該怎麼寫呢？ ─ □ ✕

Dear Ms. Sarah,

On 29 of December, 2019, the amount of 605,000 US dollars, **invoice** NO. 44767 as your **loan** payment, was **transferred** into your account. Please kindly check. I have also faxed a copy of the **remittance** slip for your reference.

Sincerely yours,

Kevin

親愛的莎拉女士：

2019年12月29日，本公司將發票號碼為44767的貨款金額605,000 美元匯入您的帳戶裡。請查收。匯款收據也已經傳真給您，以供參考。

誠摯的，

凱文

Chapter
1
Part 1
Part 2
處理訂單 Processing orders
Part 3
Part 4
Part 5
Part 6
Part 7

收到對方已付款的通知時，該怎麼回呢？ — □ ✕

Dear Kevin,

Appreciate your efficient work. I will make the delivery right away.

Yours,

Sarah

親愛的凱文：

感謝貴公司的高效率。我們會立即出貨。

真誠地，

莎拉

不同的答覆還可以怎麼回呢？ — □ ✕

Dear Kevin,

I'm afraid to tell you that as I checked our bank account just now, there's no money coming in.

Please kindly double check the bank account number and call the bank if necessary to figure it out.

Waiting for your news.

Yours,

Sarah

親愛的凱文：

我恐怕必須要告訴你，剛才我去查了我們的銀行帳戶，發現並沒有錢匯入。

請再次檢查銀行帳號，如果必要的話，請致電銀行以解決這個問題。

靜候消息。

真誠地，

莎拉

 重點單字 記起來，寫信回信超精準

① **invoice** n. 發票、出貨單
I didn't receive the invoice so I can't process the order. →我沒有收到發票，所以無法處理訂單。

② **loan** n. 借出；借出的東西；貸款 v. 借出，貸款給
The bank made a loan of ten million dollars to the factory. →銀行貸給那家工廠一千萬元。

③ **transfer** v. 轉移、轉學、換車、調職
We need to transfer at this station first.
→我們需要先在這裡轉車。

④ **remittance** n. 匯款、匯寄之款、匯款額
This payment will be made by remittance.
→這筆款項會以匯寄的方式轉給您。

Unit 16 | 入帳金額有誤

想告知**對方入帳金額錯誤**時，該怎麼寫呢？ — □ ✕

Dear Mr. Jackson,

We have received your fax of US$ 8,000.00 on 20 of April, 2020. However, I am afraid that you have **neglected** to add the cost of freight and **insurance** that was indicated on the invoice we faxed you.

We would like to ask you to wire an additional US$120.00 so that we can ship the order to you.

When receiving the full payment, we will immediately forward the goods.

Best regards,

DDC Corporation

親愛的傑克遜先生：

2020年4月20日，您傳真的8000美元到賬了，但是恐怕您忘記加上運輸和保險費用了。那些費用我們曾經在傳真給您的發票上標明了。

因此我們想請您再支付120美元運費，這樣我們就可以把貨物寄送給您了。只要收到全額貨款，我們就會立即出貨。

真誠地，

DDC 公司

DDC Corporation,

Sorry for the trouble. I will complete the missing part of the payment right away.

Regards,

Jackson

DDC 公司：

造成麻煩很抱歉。我會馬上補足款項缺少的部分。

真誠地，

傑克遜

不同的答覆還可以怎麼回呢？　　　　　— □ ✕

DDC Corporation,

I'd like to **make up for** the rest of the money and sorry for any trouble it might cause.

But I'm on a business trip; I can't transfer the money right away and we need your product in a hurry. Could you please deliver the goods first? You can **absolutely** believe in me since we've been partners for so long.

Regards,

Jackson

DDC 公司：

我會補夠不足的那部分錢，抱歉造成你們的不便。但我正在出差，不能立即為你們轉賬，而我們真的很急需你們的產品。能否先替我們出貨呢？我們合作這麼久了，你大可完全信任我。

真誠地，

傑克遜

Chapter
1

Part 1

Part 2

處理訂單 Processing orders

Part 3
Part 4
Part 5
Part 6
Part 7

重點單字記起來，寫信回信超精準

① **neglect** v./ n. 疏忽、忽視、忽略
A minor neglect may lead to a great loss.
→微小的疏忽也能導致慘重的損失。

② **insurance** n. 保險、保險費
Does the insurance cover travel expenses?
→這份保險有涵蓋旅遊支出嗎？

③ **make up for** ph. 彌補
He tried to make up for what he has done.
→他試著彌補他所做的。

④ **absolutely**
adv. 絕對地，完全地；【口】（用於對答）一點不錯，完全對
I absolutely believe in you.
→我絕對地相信你。

Unit 17 | 擬訂合約細項

想通知對方**擬訂合約**時，該怎麼寫呢？ ⊟ □ ✕

Dear Sir or Madam,

I am honored to inform you that an agreement is to be made. The detailed **specification**, unit price, quantity, **packing** and delivery of the above goods shall be provided in it. After a formal confirmation by us, a contract signed by our both sides will be **effective** then.

Please allow me remind you that this agreement serves as a legal contract.

Looking forward to hearing from you in the near future.

Yours Sincerely,

Lily

親愛的先生／女士：

我很榮幸的通知您製作一份協議。具體的要求、單價、數量、包裝及運輸要求都必須規定在協議中，並寄送給本公司。經本公司正式確認後，雙方簽訂合約，合約即刻生效。

請容許我提醒您，此協議具有法律效力。

期待近期您的回覆。

真誠地，

莉莉

Chapter

1

Part 1
Part 2

處理訂單 Processing orders

Part 3
Part 4
Part 5
Part 6
Part 7

收到對方**提醒擬訂合約**時，該怎麼回呢？ — □ ✕

Dear Lily,

Thank you for the reminder. In regard to the agreement you brought up, we will discuss about it at company's meeting tomorrow. And I will send it to you the moment it has finished.

Yours faithfully,
Charles

....

親愛的莉莉：

謝謝您的提醒。關於您所說的協議，我們公司需要明天開會討論。我將會在協議制定完成後的第一時間寄給您。

誠摯地，
查爾斯

不同的答覆還可以怎麼回呢？ — □ ✕

Dear Lily,

Thank you for your email. I am pleased to send you our agreement, which means that a **direct** cooperation relationship will be established between the two companies in the near future.

Enclosed please find a copy of our agreement.

Yours faithfully,

Charles

....

親愛的莉莉：

謝謝你的回信。我很高興寄送本公司制定的協議給您，因為這意味著我們兩公司將建立起直接的合作關係。

附件中是本公司的協議。

真誠地，

查爾斯

 重點單字記起來，寫信回信超精準

① **specification** n. 規格；詳述
Can you provide the specifications of this new product? →你能提供這個新產品的詳細規格嗎？

② **packing** n. 包裝
He's doing his packing for the trip tomorrow.
→他為了明天的旅行收拾行李。

③ **effective** adj. 有效的；（法律等）生效的，起作用的
The lockdown of the city will be effective from tomorrow. →封城將會從明天開始生效。

④ **direct** adj. 直接的
His remarks were not directed at you.
→他的話不是針對你的。

Unit 18 | 制定參考協議

Dear Sir/ Madam,

This is Taiwan Good Company. It's been two months since we visited your company last time in the U.S. During this period, our company had seriously had some discussions and reviewed the **vinyl** player produced by your company. Now, we think that this product is most likely to enjoy **popularity** in Taiwan. So, we want to import it and sell it in Taiwan. It will be highly appreciated if you could make an agreement and send it to us for reference. You can add all related items in this agreement so that we can further discuss about the importing details. Thanks.

Yours,

Yang

親愛的先生／女士：

我們是台灣貨品公司。自上次在美國參觀貴公司已經兩個月了。這段期間裡，本公司認真討論研究了貴公司生產的黑膠播放器。現在我們認為，這款電子產品在台灣會大受歡迎，所以，我們想進口貴公司的產品，然後在台灣販售。希望貴公司能制定一份協議書，並發給本公司以供參考。請加入所有相關條款，以便我們進一步商談進口事宜。謝謝。

真誠地，

楊

Dear Yang,

Thanks for your e-mail. We are glad that you are interested in the new vinyl player.

Enclosed is the agreement we made about the cooperation, inclusive of importing details, price, and so on. If you need other information, please do not **hesitate** to contact us. We will reply to you as soon as possible. We hope that we can enjoy a happy cooperation. Thanks.

Best regards,

Lewis

親愛的楊：

感謝您的郵件。很高興您對新的黑膠播放器感興趣。

附件中是本公司針對合作所制定的協議，包含進口細節及價格等細項。如果您還需要其他資訊，請隨時聯繫我們。本公司會盡快回覆您。希望我們能合作愉快。謝謝。

真誠地，

路易斯

Dear Yang,

We are very **delighted** to receive your e-mail and to know your interest in our new product.

Would you please tell us your company address? We will send the agreement to your company as soon as the agreement is finished.

Chapter

1

Part 1

Part 2

處理訂單 Processing orders

Part 3

Part 4

Part 5

Part 6

Part 7

Please feel free to contact us if you need other information. May we have a pleasant cooperation. Thanks.

Best regards,

Lewis

親愛的楊：

很高興收到您的郵件以及得知您對本公司的新產品有興趣。

您可以把貴公司的地址告訴我們嗎？協議書一制定好我們會立即寄給您。

如果您還需要其他資訊，請隨時和我們聯繫。希望我們能合作愉快。謝謝。

真誠地，

路易斯

 重點單字記起來，寫信回信超精準

① **vinyl** n. 黑膠
My dad bought the vinyl of his favorite band yesterday. →我爸昨天買了他最喜歡的樂團的黑膠唱片。

② **popularity** n. 普及，流行；大眾化
The infamous singer is losing his popularity.
→這個惡名昭彰的歌手漸漸不受歡迎。

③ **hesitate** v. 猶豫、躊躇
Don't hesitate for too long, or else you might miss the opportunity. →別猶豫太久，不然你可能會錯失機會。

④ **delighted** adj. 高興的，快樂的
He was very much delighted with the results.
→他對這個結果感到非常滿意。

Unit 19 | 寄回書面合約

需要對方先**寄回合約**時，該怎麼寫呢？ ⊖ ▢ ✕

Dear Sir/ Madam,

I'm Kate from American Goods Company. Last Friday, we sent you an agreement about the importing of our vinyl player upon your request.

This morning, our country has **adjusted exporting** tax, which will affect the related items in the agreement. So, would you please send the agreement back to us within this week? We will return it to you after we fix the tax issue with our government. We are deeply sorry and we promise you a 10% discount for all the products. Thanks.

Best regards,

Kate

⋯⋯⋯⋯⋯⋯⋯⋯⋯⋯⋯⋯⋯⋯⋯⋯⋯⋯⋯⋯⋯⋯⋯⋯⋯⋯⋯⋯⋯⋯⋯

親愛的先生／女士：

我是美國貨品公司的凱特。上週五應貴公司要求，本公司寄給您一份關於本公司黑膠播放器的協議書。

今天早晨，我國調整了出口稅，這將會影響到協議書中的相關條款。所以貴公司能否在本週之內將協議書寄給本公司？本公司與政府協商確定稅率問題後會立即將協議書寄回貴公司。非常抱歉以及本公司承諾所有產品本公司將給您9折優惠。謝謝。

真誠地，

凱特

Chapter
1

Part 1
Part 2

處理訂單 Processing orders

Part 3
Part 4
Part 5
Part 6
Part 7

收到對方**要求先寄回合約**的請求時，該怎麼回呢？ — □ ✕

Dear Kate,

We did receive the agreement from your company yesterday. We are delighted at the discount. However, time is so limited that we do not even have a chance to read the agreement. We are afraid that we may not be able to send you the agreement within this week. The earliest day may be next Tuesday. We are sorry for this, and hope that it would not bring you any trouble. Thanks.

Best regards,

Wang

親愛的凱特：

本公司昨天確實收到了貴公司寄來的協議書。很高興您提供我方折扣。但是，由於時間緊迫，我們還未來得及閱讀此協議書，恐怕沒辦法在本週內寄給你們。最早應該下週二可以寄給貴公司。很抱歉，希望沒給貴公司帶來麻煩。謝謝。

真誠地，

王

不同的答覆還可以怎麼回呢？ — □ ✕

Dear Kate,

Thanks for your discount. We really appreciate that.

We received your agreement two days ago. Yesterday, we **copied** the agreement for every manager and discussed it within the company. So, we can send this agreement to you this afternoon and hope that you could receive it within this week. Please let us know the **modifications**. Thanks.

Best regards,

Wang

親愛的凱特：

我們非常感謝貴公司給的優惠。

我們在兩天前收到協議書。昨天已經複印並發給各個經理，也已經在公司內部商討過了。所以，今天下午我們把協議書寄給你們，希望能在本週內收到。如有修改，請告知。謝謝。

真誠地，

王

重點單字記起來，寫信回信超精準

① **adjust** v. 調整、調節
Let's adjust the machine to make it function more smoothly. →我們來調整一下機器使其能更順暢地運作。

② **export** v. 輸出，出品 n. 出口；傳播
The cash crop export is very important to this country. →經濟作物的出口對這個國家是非常重要的。

③ **copy** n. 抄本，副本；複製品 v. 抄寫；複製
I will send you a copy of the letter.
→我將把信件的副本寄給你。

④ **modification** n. 修改；改正
Some urgent modifications need to be made in this proposal. →這個企劃裡頭需要緊急做一些修改。

Note

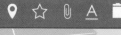

Unit 01 | 商標註冊申請

Dear Secretary of CAAC (Civil Aviation Administration of Taiwan),

I, Mike Lee, hereby apply for a license to show the **trademark**, "Level A Service," for our airline headquarter located in Beijing to use.

This application is in accordance with the **regulations** of the CAAC. I understand the regulations of CAAC that govern the display of said trademark and the relevant manner of conducting business and I agree to obey such regulations at all times.

Sincerely yours,

Mike Lee

親愛的台灣民航協會會長：

本人，麥可‧李，特此寫信申請商標使用許可證，讓位於北京的航空公司的總部便可以獲准使用「Level A Service」商標。

本申請係依據台灣民航協會條例提出。本人理解協會對上述商標使用和相關業務經營模式的規範條例，並同意永久遵守這些條例。

真誠地，

麥可‧李

Chapter
1

Part 1
Part 2
Part 3

疑難雜症 Common situations

Part 4
Part 5
Part 6
Part 7

收到**商標申請信**時，該怎麼回呢？　　— □ ✕

Mr. Lee,

Please provide us the official application form, attached with this letter, and then we can go to the next step.

If you have any further inquiries, please don't hesitate to let me know.

Yours sincerely,

Jonas Sharp

Secretary of CAAC

李先生：

請填寫正式的申請表格，並附上這封郵件一起寄給我們，以進入申請的下一階段。

有任何進一步詢問請與我聯繫。

真誠地，

強納斯・夏普

台灣民航協會

不同的答覆還可以怎麼回呢？　　— □ ✕

Dear Mike,

I'm afraid you have to **suspend** this application because we're going to alter the usage of the trademark in the coming **convention** of CAAC.

Please be patient until the conclusion draws out.

Yours,

Jonas Sharp

Secretary of CAAC

親愛的麥可：

恐怕你們這份申請要暫時擱置，因為在即將舉行的CAAC大會上我們要修改有關商標使用的內容。

請耐心的等待結果。

真誠地，

強納斯‧夏普

台灣民航協會

 重點單字記起來，寫信回信超精準

① **trademark** n. 商標
The trademark of KLM is highly similar to that of HJS.
→KLM 和 HJS 的商標高度相像。

② **regulation** n. 規則、規範
The new labor regulations are absurd!
→新的勞工規範簡直荒謬！

③ **suspend** v. 懸吊、懸掛、延緩
The construction was suspended due to the disease control. →因防疫，建造工程暫時停止。

④ **convention** n. 大會、協定、習俗、慣例
Not all social conventions are rational and needed to obey. →並不是所有社會習俗都是理性且被遵守的。

Unit 02 訂單取消失敗

沒有**及時取消訂單**時，該怎麼寫呢？ — □ ✕

Dear Sir or Madam,

We are terribly sorry for failing to **cancel** your order in time. This was our mistake and we will accept the **return** of the goods. We understand the inconvenience our **oversight** must be causing you and we can ensure you that we will be more careful next time and such an error won't happen again.

Yours sincerely,

AP Co.

親愛的先生／女士：

未能及時取消貴公司的訂單，我們感到非常抱歉。這是我們的錯誤，我們接受貴公司的退貨。很抱歉給您造成不便，我們保證以後會加倍小心，避免此類錯誤再次發生。

真誠地，

AP 公司

Dear Sir or Madam,

I'm glad to receive your letter regarding the failure to cancel our order. We accept your apology. Since it was a mistake on your own system, we'd like to claim for related **compensation** for the inconvenience it had caused. At the same time, we really hope this kind of mistake can be avoided next time.

Truly yours,

PC Co.

親愛的先生／女士：

我們已經收到貴公司關於此次未能及時取消訂單的郵件。我們接受貴公司的道歉。既然此次過失是由貴公司系統故障所導致，我們將向貴公司提出相關賠償要求。同時，我們希望此類錯誤今後不再發生。

真誠地，

PC公司

Dear Sir or Madam,

Your letter about the failure regarding our order cancelation has explained the possible reason about this matter; we accept your apology on this issue. However, we will still ask for certain compensation for the loss you have caused, and we hope that this error will not happen again.

Truly yours,

PC Co.

Chapter

1

Part 1

Part 2

Part 3

疑難雜症 Common situations

Part 4

Part 5

Part 6

Part 7

親愛的先生／女士：

貴公司關於此次未能及時取消訂單事宜的郵件，我們已經收到，並且瞭解了相關的原因，我們接受你們的道歉。不過，我們仍將請貴公司就相關損失進行賠償。同時希望以後這種情況不再發生。

真誠地，

PC公司

 重點單字 記起來，寫信回信超精準

① **cancel** v. 取消、刪去
The meeting was canceled because the clients failed to make it on time.

→因客戶無法準時到場，會議取消了。

② **return** v. 返還、送回
Please return the package to the sender.

→請把此包裹退給寄件人。

③ **oversight** n. 疏忽，紕漏
We should all learn from this oversight that cost us great losses.

→我們都應從此造成巨大損失的紕漏中學習。

④ **compensation** n. 賠償、補償
I didn't get any compensation when I was dismissed.

→我被解雇的時候沒有拿到任何補償金。

Unit 03 | 拒絕延遲交貨

想要拒絕對方提出**延遲交貨**的要求時，該怎麼寫呢？ ▬ ☐ ✕

Dear Mr. White,

I'm afraid that we can't accept your request to delay the delivery.

We are in urgent need of those components, or our factory has to stop production process and therefore we can't meet our customer's **deadline**. If you can not deliver them on time, we shall have no choice but to cancel the order and place our order to another company. We are really very sorry for it.

Thank you for your understanding.

Yours sincerely,

John Smith

親愛的懷特先生：

很遺憾，本公司恐怕無法接受貴公司所要求的延遲交貨。

我們目前急需這些零件，否則，我們的工廠就不得不停工，我們將無法在截止日期前完工。如果貴公司無法準時交貨，那麼我們沒有別的選擇，只好取消我們的訂單，把訂單交給其他的公司。對此我們非常抱歉。

敬請諒解！

真誠地，

約翰・史密斯

Chapter

1

Part 1

Part 2

Part 3

疑難雜症 Common situations

Part 4

Part 5

Part 6

Part 7

收到對方**拒絕延遲出貨**的信時，該怎麼回呢？ — □ ✕

Dear Mr. Smith,

Please accept our sincere apologies for the delay of delivery.

The delay was due to the **upgrade** of equipment and we guarantee that this renewal could make our components more outstanding in the future.

We hope you will forgive our delay and continue in purchasing products from our company since we have the most advanced manufacturing equipment. Sincerely wish you consider to cooperate with us again.

Truly yours,

Mike White

親愛的史密斯先生：

關於延遲出貨一事，請接受我最誠摯的歉意。

此次延誤是由於我們對設備進行了升級。我們確定，此次更新能夠讓我們的產品在未來表現更加出色。

希望貴公司能夠原諒我們的延誤，並繼續購買我們的產品，因為我們擁有最先進的設備，真誠希望您再次考慮與我們合作。

真誠地，

麥克‧懷特

不同的答覆還可以怎麼回呢？ — □ ✕

Dear Mr. Smith,

Your letter of 10th, August, 2020 has had our attention.

We required delaying the delivery before; it is due to certain circumstances that are beyond our control now. Now, improvement has been made, and the shipping company has promised to give us priority in their **transportation** arrangement. The goods are believed to arrive in time.

Please accept our sincere apology for the confusion you have been caused.

Faithfully yours,

Mike White

親愛的史密斯先生：

我們已經看到您2020年8月10寄來的郵件！

我們先前要求延遲出貨，那是因為當時情況已經超出我們所能控制的範圍。不過，現在情況已經有所改善，運輸公司答應優先安排運輸我們的貨物。這批貨應該會準時抵達。

給您帶來困擾，我們深表歉意！

真誠地，

麥克‧懷特

重點單字 記起來，寫信回信超精準

① **deadline** n. 截止日期
The deadline of the essay is next Sunday.
→下週日是論文的截止日期。

② **upgrade** v. 升級、提升
The equipment failed to function properly because we didn't upgrade the software.
→因為我們沒有升級軟體，設備無法正常運作。

③ **transportation** n. 運輸、運送
You'll have to take public transportation because I have to work tomorrow.
→因為我明天要工作，你要自己搭大眾運輸工具。

Unit 04 | 提早出貨要求

對方希望**提早出貨**的要求時，該怎麼寫呢？ — □ ✕

Dear Sir or Madam,

We have received your e-mail requesting the early delivery of the goods. After checking on the delivery schedule, we find that there is no possibility to shift the time of delivery to an earlier date. We have done our best to meet your request but it usually takes three weeks to finish the whole process. Thank you for your understanding.

Yours sincerely,

Tom

....

親愛的先生／女士：

我們已經收到你們要求提前出貨的郵件。我們已經確認了出貨進度，但是無法提前給您供貨。我們已經盡最大努力交貨，但是整個流程通常都會需要三週的時間來完成。敬請諒解。

真誠地，

湯姆

Dear Sir or Madam,

As we mentioned in our last letter, we are in **urgent** need of the goods. And if you are not able to **supply** them in accordance with our request, we then have no other choice but to seek an **alternative** source of supply.

Yours sincerely,

Tony

親愛的先生／女士：

正如我們致貴公司的電子郵件中所提到的，我們急需此批貨物。如果貴公司未能及時供貨，我們可能被迫尋求其他貨源。

真誠地，

東尼

Dear Sir or Madam,

Thank you for your letter telling us the exact time to deliver the goods. As we have mentioned in our last letter, we are in urgent need of these goods, and if you cannot **adjust** the arrival date we request, we should negotiate another date so that both of us can settle the inconvenience. Then, is 20th of August a good time for you? Hope to receive your reply as soon as possible.

Yours sincerely,

Tony

Chapter

1

Part 1

Part 2

Part 3

疑難雜症 Common situations

Part 4

Part 5

Part 6

Part 7

親愛的先生／女士：

謝謝您在郵件中告知我們確切的出貨時間。不過，正如我們在上一封郵件當中提到的一樣，我們急需此批貨品。如果你們無法按照我們的要求調整到貨時間的話，那我們應協商出另一個雙方都能接受的時間，以免造成雙方的困擾，那麼8月20日是否可行，盼望您的回覆。

真誠地，

東尼

 重點單字記起來，寫信回信超精準

① **urgent** n. 緊急的、迫切的
Many people in the Europe are in urgent need of masks now. →現在歐洲許多人急需口罩。

② **supply** v. 供應、提供
Can you ask them to supply the goods in time?
→你能要求他們準時提供商品嗎？

③ **alternative** n. 選擇、供選擇之物　adj. 其他的、另類的
The only alternative I have now is to transfer to another school.
→我現在唯一的選擇就是轉學。

④ **adjust** v. 調整
I slightly adjust my schedule so that I can work a part-time job.
→我微調了我的行程，以便我能兼職。

Unit 05 | 臨時取消訂單

Dear Sir or Madam,

In accordance with our contract, we can cancel the order only if you inform us two weeks **prior** to the delivery date. However, you just did it without informing us in advance. We **persist** in doing business in accordance with the contract; we have to ask you to stick to the contract. Besides, you should give us a satisfactory explanation for the matter mentioned above.

Yours sincerely,

Paul

親愛的先生／女士：

根據合約規定，我們只能接受出貨日期前兩週的訂單取消要求。然而，貴公司未提前通知就取消了訂單。我們公司一向嚴格按照合約行事，我們必須要求你們也按照合約行事。此外，也希望貴公司能夠就此事提出一個能令人滿意的解釋。

真誠地，

保羅

Chapter

1

Part 1
Part 2
Part 3

疑難雜症 Common situations

Part 4
Part 5
Part 6
Part 7

對方**無法按要求取消**訂單時，該怎麼回呢？ — ☐ ✕

Dear Sir or Madam,

We are terribly sorry about this matter. Some technical issues occurred in our factories, and our **technicians** and engineers are all working day-and-night to solve the manufacturing crisis. Unfortunately, based on experts' predictions, it won't be solved until at least two weeks later since we need to import other components for the **malfunctioning** machines.

Hope we can continue our collaboration in the future.

Yours sincerely,

AP Co

親愛的先生／女士：

對於此事我們感到非常抱歉。我們工廠出現了一些技術問題，技師和工程師都日以繼夜地想要解決此製程危機。不幸的是，專業人士預估，此問題至少兩週內都還無法解決，因為我們需要替無法正常運作的機器進口其他零件。

希望未來我們能持續合作。

真誠地，

AP 公司

不同的答覆還可以怎麼回呢？ — ☐ ✕

Dear Sir or Madam,

Please forgive us for not cancelling your order in time. We will take responsibility for the error. We have instructed the department in charge to be more careful next time and make sure such an error will not happen again. Please accept our apologies for any inconvenience it caused you.

Yours sincerely,

Tony

親愛的先生／女士：

未能即時取消您的訂單，我們感到非常抱歉。我們會為這次的過失負責任。我們已經指示相關部門以後多加注意，並確保此類錯誤不再發生。給您帶來諸多不便，請接受我們誠摯的歉意。

真誠地，

東尼

 重點單字記起來，寫信回信超精準

① **prior** adj. 先前的、居前的
The contract has to be final prior to the opening ceremony. →在開幕儀式之前，合約必須完成。

② **persist** v. 堅持、持續
I persist in completing my duties before I resign.
→在我離職之前，我堅持完成我的職務。

③ **technician** n. 技工、技師
We decide to hire more technician to enhance our quality. →我們決定雇用更多技師以提升品質。

④ **malfunction** n. 故障、無法使用
The sudden malfunction of the machine cost us dearly. →機器突然故障讓我們損失重大。

Unit 06 | 變更會議時間

Hello Mervi,

It's our pleasure to have your visit in our company last week. During the three days, many **technical** details in operation procedures are becoming clearer to us under your kind and specific instructions. We are also honored to receive your **compliment** e-mail.

For the date of our next **teleconference**, you suggested 8th of Nov., but I am afraid I might not be available then as I have another team of customer visit on that day. So, could you please check if it is possible for us to hold this meeting at the same time on 9th of Nov.? Sorry for the inconvenience. Please let me know if this is **feasible** for you and your team. Thanks in advance.

Kind regards,
Cecilia

- -

莫威，你好：

您上週能到訪本公司，我們深感榮幸。在3天的參訪過程中，您熱心仔細的指導讓我們對許多操作程序上的具體技術細節有了更詳細的理解。收到您的讚許，更讓我們十分榮幸。

您建議我們下次電話會議的日期訂在11月8日。但是由於當天有另一組客戶來訪，我很可能無法參加。所以可否請您將會議安排至11月9日的同一時段？為此帶來不便，我感到抱歉。請回覆此時間對您及您的團隊是否方便。謝謝。

真誠地，
西西莉亞

Dear Cecilia,

Thank you for your e-mail. I am also very thankful for all the arrangements you have made. What's more important, the whole trial process has been going quite smoothly under everyone's effort. For the time of our next con-call, 9th of Nov. looks ok for me. Anyway, I will check with Sirkka and let you know our decision as soon as possible.

I will come back to you later.

Best wishes!

Mervi

親愛的西西莉亞：

感謝你的來信。非常感謝你為我們的訪問所做的一切安排。更重要的是，在大家的共同努力下，我們的測試過程進行的非常順利。對於我們下次電話會議的時間，改到11月9日我沒有問題。但是我需要和舍卡確認一下再回覆你。

稍後再與你聯繫。

真誠地，

莫威

Dear Cecilia,

Thank you very much for your pre-notice. I have confirmed with Sirkka and other staff, and the meeting, 9th of Nov. is ok for everyone. So, let's set our next con-call at 9:00AM (GMT +8:00). I will update the meeting invitation to all later today. Please kindly check when you receive it and make preparations accordingly.

Chapter
1

Part 1
Part 2
Part 3

疑難雜症 Common situations

Part 4
Part 5
Part 6
Part 7

Let's talk more about the cooperation details during our teleconference. Have a nice day!

Yours Sincerely,

Mervi

親愛的西西莉亞：

謝謝你提前通知。我已經和舍卡與其他與會人員確認過了，大家都可以在11月9日出席會議。所以我們的會議時間將改為11月9日上午九點（GMT +8:00）開始。我今天會更新會議邀請給大家。請查收邀請並作相應的準備。

我們在會議中再詳談合作細節吧。希望你今天過得愉快！

真誠地，

莫威

 重點單字記起來，寫信回信超精準

① **technical** adj. 技術（上）的、科技的
This is a technical problem that after-sale services won't cover. →這是售後服務無法處理的技術問題。

② **compliment** v. 讚美、嘉許 n. 讚美的話
My manager complimented me for my performance.
→我的主管讚許我的表現。

③ **teleconference** n. 遠端電話會議
The annual teleconference should take place next month. →年度遠端電話會議應於下個月舉行。

④ **feasible** adj. 合理的、可行的
This plan is far from feasible and should be rewritten at once. →此計畫完全不可行，應立即重寫。

Unit 07 | 要求產品退貨

要向對方**提出退貨要求**時，該怎麼寫呢？ ─ □ ✕

Dear Paul:

Thanks for the long-term kind support.

I am sorry to inform you that the latest batch of parts delivered at our plant on 16 of Sep. did not pass our quality check. Failure rate is around 24%. In this case, we have no other choice but **reject** this batch. You can find in the attached data and photos the status of these goods. Please help checking other in-transit goods and your inventory if they are in the same production with this one. Also, please offer updated delivery schedule based on your improvement.

Looking forward to your reply soon.

Best wishes,

Michael

保羅您好：

感謝您長期以來的支持。

很遺憾的通知你，貴公司於9月16日寄達本公司廠區的貨品並未通過本公司的品質檢驗。不良率在24% 左右。因此，我們只能作退貨處理。透過附件資料與照片你可以看到更多關於此批貨物的資訊，請幫忙查驗在運送途中的貨物和貴公司庫存是否和此批產品為同一生產批次，並請提供改善後的交貨計畫。

早覆為盼！

真誠地，

麥可

Chapter

1

Part 1

Part 2

Part 3

疑難雜症 Common situations

Part 4

Part 5

Part 6

Part 7

收到對方**要求退貨**的信時，該怎麼回呢？ — □ ✕

Dear Michael,

Thanks for **highlighting** this issue timely. I have **thoroughly** checked the files you offered and still found some points that need a mutual discussion. I will make an on-site visit next Tuesday. Hope we can find some better ways to deal with this batch of parts.

Sorry for the inconvenience this has brought to your company. I will follow up with staff concerned on this issue.

Yours Sincerely,

Paul

親愛的麥可：

感謝您及時提出此問題。我已仔細查看您提供的資料和圖片，發現有一些問題仍需雙方討論。下週二我會到貴公司拜訪，希望到時我們可以找到更好的辦法來處理此批貨物。

我對此產生困擾感到抱歉。後續我會緊密與相關人員跟進此事。

真誠地，

保羅

不同的答覆還可以怎麼回呢？ — □ ✕

Dear Michael,

Thank you very much for the notification. I am glad that finally we can reach this step where we can arrange on-site sorting and reworking for this batch of flawed goods. Of course, the remained NG parts can be **disposed** of immediately. We can arrange a new delivery to cover those. As for the problems discovered in this batch, we will of certainly find its root cause and try every method to prevent it from happening again. Thanks again for your kind support to organize a meeting for both parties and settling this issue successfully.

Yours Sincerely,

Paul

親愛的麥可：

非常感謝你的通知。值得高興的是，我們終於可以達成一致共識，安排此批待工產品的場內挑選與重製。當然，剩餘的不良品可直接報廢，我們可以安排一批新的貨作為替代。對於此次發現的問題，我們一定會查明根本原因，盡力避免再次發生。再次感謝您幫忙召集雙方會議並成功解決此問題。

真誠地，

保羅

 重點單字 記起來，寫信回信超精準

① **reject** v. 拒絕、捨棄、排斥、退出
You should press the "reject" button before you pull out the USB.
→在拔出USB之前，你應該先按「退出」的按鈕。

② **highlight** v. 強調、照亮 n. 突出的部分
Underline the first two lines to highlight the key points. →將前兩行畫底線以凸顯重點。

③ **thoroughly** adv. 十分地、徹底地
We always examine the products thoroughly before we ship them. →在出貨前，我們總是徹底檢查商品。

④ **dispose** v. 處理、處置、配置
My mom wanted to disposed of all my old books.
→我媽媽想要丟掉我所有的舊書。

Unit 08 | 收到產品投訴

收到顧客**投訴產品瑕疵**時，該怎麼寫呢？

Dear Mr. Smith,

On behalf of Wal-Mart Shopping Mall, I, Ms. Abby Sun, the Customer Relation Manager, sincerely apologies to you.

As we receive a notice from your side that you had purchase an **expired** peanut butter from our company. We hereby inform you that this was unintentional. The one you purchased from our mall might be mistakenly placed during the packaging.

Therefore, to show our sincerity to solve this problem, we'll pay for the fine amount mentioned by you in your notice. We also enclose herewith a gift as compensation for the inconvenience we caused to you.

We apologize for the inconvenience.

Yours faithfully,
Ms. Abby Sun
Customer Relation Manager, Wal-Mart shopping mall

親愛的史密斯先生：

我是沃爾瑪超市的客戶部經理，孫艾比。我謹代表我們超市向您致上歉意。

您來函說您在我們超市購買到了一罐過期的花生醬。這可能是我們的無心之過。您買到那一瓶很可能是廠商在包裝時不小心混進去的。

為展現解決問題的誠意，我們會支出您在通知信中提及的賠償金額。隨函附上一份小禮物，謹作為給您帶來的不便的小小補償。

我們對於我們的過失表示歉意。

真誠地，
孫艾比 女士
沃爾瑪超市客戶部經理

Dear Ms. Sun,

Thank you for your **prompt** reply to my complaint letter. I appreciate your sincere apology for the mistake you made and your thoughtful gift.

Taking your explanation into consideration, I do accept your apology for this unpleasant incident.

As I enjoy purchasing daily **necessities** in your Mall, I do hope this undesirable incident will not stand in the way of my future purchase.

I expect to purchase more cheap and fine **commodities** form Wal-Mart.

Yours,

Jon Smith

親愛的孫女士：

感謝你對我的投訴信回覆及時。很高興收到你們的道歉以及你們精心準備的小禮物。

再三考慮過你們的解釋，我確實能夠接受你們對我造成的不愉快的道歉。

我非常喜歡在你們超市購買生活日用品，希望此事不會對我今後在你們超市的消費造成影響。

我期待在沃爾瑪買到更多物美價廉的商品。

真誠地，

強・史密斯

不同的答覆還可以怎麼回呢？　　　　— □ ✕

Dear Ms. Sun,

Thank you for your apology message dated 12th of July, 2020.

Although I appreciate your sincere apology and the thoughtful gift, your explanation seems unsatisfactory to me as I have bought two different expired commodities from Wal-mart last

Chapter
1

Part 1
Part 2
Part 3

疑難雜症 Common situations

Part 4
Part 5
Part 6
Part 7

month. How can you possibly explain this? My long-time trust in your products turns out to be a mistake.

Your reasonable explanation is still expected.

Yours,

Jon Smith

親愛的孫女士：

您於2020年7月12日的道歉信已收悉。

儘管我很感謝你的道歉以及你們精心挑選的禮物，對於我在上個月買到兩次過期產品，你要如何解釋？我長期以來一直信任沃爾瑪所出售的商品，現在看起來是個錯誤。

你需要作出更合理的解釋。

真誠地，

強・史密斯

 **重點單字**記起來，寫信回信超精準

① **expire** v. 到期、（期限）終止
The contract will expire next month and we'd like to renew it. →合約下個月將會到期，我們想要續約。

② **prompt** adj. 即刻的、立即的
We should take prompt actions before it's too late.
→我們應採取即刻行動才不會為時已晚。

③ **necessity** n. 必需性、必需品
I didn't feel the necessity to buy a new refrigerator for the moment. →我不覺得現在有需要買一個新冰箱。

④ **commodity** n. 商品；日常用品
The commodity price of cosmetics usually falls between 200 to 300 NTD.
→化妝品的商品價格大約落在 200 到 300 台幣之間。

Unit 09 | 未能收到發票

發現沒有收到**開立的發票**時，該怎麼寫呢？ ─ □ ✕

Dear Sir or Madam,

We are delighted to inform you that the goods arrived in Taipei yesterday morning. However, there is no formal **Commercial** Invoice attached. We have searched the cartons thoroughly and nothing was found. Please mail the Invoice immediately for **customs** purpose. We sincerely hope this kind of situation will not happen again since it brought us a lot of troubles in customs clearance. We are looking forward to receiving your Commercial Invoice soon.

Sincerely Yours,

Tom Green

親愛的先生／女士：

很高興在此通知您我們在貴公司訂購的貨物已於昨日早上抵達台北。不過，我們卻沒有正式的商業發票。我們已經仔細查找了裝貨物的箱子，都沒有找到。請立即將發票寄予我們，以便通關。我們衷心的希望這樣的情況不會再發生，它已經給我們在海關通關時造成了莫大的困擾。期待能夠盡快收到貴公司的商業發票。

真誠地，

湯姆・格林

Part 1

Part 2

Part 3

疑難雜症 Common situations

Part 4

Part 5

Part 6

Part 7

收到對方知會**未收到發票**的信時，該怎麼回呢？ — ☐ ✕

Dear Sir or Madam,

I am **extremely** sorry to tell you that, as you pointed out, a mistake has been made on the invoice. I do apologize for any inconvenience it may cause. We have taken immediate action to issue the invoice and send it to you by express delivery the moment we received your email.

We have taken measures to **ensure** that such an error will not happen again.

Yours sincerely,

PC Co

親愛的先生／女士：

非常抱歉的告訴您，正像您指出的，此次貨物的發票沒有及時附上。我們為此給您帶來的不便向您道歉。收到您的郵件後，我們已經第一時間開好發票並用快遞寄給您了。

我們已經採取相關措施以確保此類錯誤不會再發生。

真誠地，

PC 公司

不同的答覆還可以怎麼回呢？ — ☐ ✕

Dear Sir or Madam,

Please accept our sincere apology for the inconvenience that may cause. We feel terribly sorry for the invoice error. We were embarrassed to discover that your invoice was misplaced in another set of goods. I have instructed our financial staff to issue a new invoice to you by express delivery. We will make certain that all delivery is made correctly in the future.

Yours,

PC Co

親愛的先生／女士：

對於此次發票的事情給你們帶來的不便我們感到非常抱歉。非常尷尬的是我們發現貴公司的發票被附送到另一批貨物了。我們已經通知了財務人員立即透過快遞新開的發票寄送至貴公司。我們今後一定確保所有貨物將正確送達。

真誠地，

PC 公司

 重點單字記起來，寫信回信超精準

① **commercial** adj. 商業（性）的 n. 廣告
This a video is for commercial use only.
→此部影片僅作為商業用途。

② **customs** n. 海關、關稅
After I got through customs, I saw my parents waving at me. →一過海關，我便看到父母正在向我招手。

③ **extremely** adv. 極度地
I was extremely angry at his hurtful remarks.
→我因他傷人的話語感到極度生氣。

④ **ensure** v. 確保、確使
You need to ensure that no one gets hurt in this activity. →你必須確保沒有人會在此活動中受傷。

Unit 10 發票誤開致歉

發現開立**錯誤發票**時，該怎麼寫呢？

Dear Sir or Madam,

Regretfully, I have to inform you that the receipt we sent to you on 23 of September was mistaken.

The mistake was made by our new accountant who was **recruited** recently and was lack of experience in this area. We apologize for the inconvenience caused by our error.

We will send you the correct formal receipt as soon as possible.

Sincerely yours,

Tony

親愛的先生：

很遺憾的告知貴公司，本公司於9月23日寄送給您的發票開錯了。

由於新招募的會計師缺乏相關經驗，於是出現了這樣的錯誤。很抱歉因為我們的疏忽給貴公司帶來了不便。

本公司將儘快寄出正確的發票。

真誠地，

東尼

Dear Tony,

Glad to receive your e-mail with regard to the wrongly-**addressed** receipt. It did cause some confusions on our part. We just wish to receive the correct receipt and return the former one. We will continue buying products from your company since we have established a good partnership. I also believe that similar mistake will not happen in the future.

Sincerely yours,

William

親愛的湯尼：

很高興收到你澄清開錯發票的郵件。它的確給我方帶來一些困惑。現在我們希望收到正確的發票並且退回原發票。由於我們已經建立了良好的互利貿易關係，我們將繼續向您購買貨物。我相信類似的過失不會在我們未來的交易中出現。

真誠地，

威廉

Dear Tony,

It is a great **relief** to receive your e-mail about the receipt we received days earlier.

The amount of money we paid on August 20 is $80000 but in the receipt we received shows $8000. We hope to receive another receipt about the remaining $72000 or return the receipt and get the correct one. Your early reply will be appreciated.

Sincerely
William

Chapter

1

Part 1

Part 2

Part 3

疑難雜症 Common situations

Part 4

Part 5

Part 6

Part 7

親愛的湯尼：

本公司很寬慰能收到關於本公司日前收到的錯誤發票説明郵件。

在8月20日，本公司支付了八萬美元，而發票上顯示的卻是八千美元。本公司希望收到關於另外七萬兩千的發票，或者我們退回錯誤發票，換取正確的。儘早回覆將不勝感激。

真誠地，

威廉

 重點單字 記起來，寫信回信超精準

① **regretfully** adv. 痛惜地、遺憾地
Regretfully, I must reject this generous offer.
→很抱歉，我不得不拒絕此慷慨的提議。

② **recruit** n. 徵募、吸收（新成員）
Our company recruited 50 new engineers last year.
→去年我們公司招募了五十名新工程師。

③ **address** v. 註明地址、致詞 n. 地址
Can you check if the address on this package is correct?
→你能確認一下包裹上的地址是否正確嗎？

④ **relief** n. 寬慰、鬆口氣
What a great relief!
→真是鬆了一口氣！

Unit 11 | 延遲匯款致歉

知會將**逾期匯款**想道歉時，該怎麼寫呢？

Dear Sir or Madam,

We are terribly sorry for the late **remittance** this time and the inconvenience this matter has given you. Our company's new design is under production and we are facing the issue of the shortage of fund this time. However, the situation will not last long. Anyway, please accept our **earnest** apology. We can ensure you that you will receive the remittance on time in the future. We appreciate it very much for your understanding.

Yours faithfully,

Tom

親愛的先生／女士：

有關這次的逾期匯款給您造成的不便，我們感到非常抱歉。由於我們公司近期的新產品正處於生產期，須面對資金短缺，但是這種情況不久就會好轉的。無論如何，請接受我們誠摯的歉意。我們保證以後一定會準時匯款。非常感謝您的理解。

真誠地，

湯姆

Chapter

1

Part 1
Part 2
Part 3

疑難雜症 Common situations

Part 4
Part 5
Part 6
Part 7

收到對方知會將**逾期匯款**的信時，該怎麼回呢？ — □ ×

Dear Sir or Madam,

As you are usually very prompt in settling your accounts, at first we are **wondering** whether there is any special reason why we have not received the payment of the goods. However, your letter has explained the cause clearly, and we totally understand your situation. Still, we wish that you could settle the problem as soon as possible.

Yours sincerely,

Tony

親愛的先生／女士：

鑒於貴公司總是及時結清貨款，而此次逾期未收到貴公司上批次貨物的匯款，我們原先正疑惑是否有任何特殊原因。不過，你們的郵件已經詳細解釋了相關原因，我們完全能夠理解你們當前的狀況。依然希望你們能夠早日解決相關問題。

真誠地，

東尼

不同的答覆還可以怎麼回呢？ — □ ×

Dear Sir or Madam,

It has been several weeks since we sent you our first invoice and we have not received your payment yet. We were wondering about your plans for paying your account. And your letter has explained the possible reason; we **completely** understand your situation. However, we must now ask you to settle this account within two months.

Truly yours,

Tony

親愛的先生／女士：

我們的第一份發票已經寄出好幾個星期，但我們尚未收到您的任何款項。我想瞭解一下貴公司的付款計畫。您的來信已經說明了詳細的原因，我們能充分理解。但是，請貴公司務必在兩個月內結清這筆款項。

真誠地，

東尼

 重點單字記起來，寫信回信超精準

① **remittance** n. 匯款
Have they received your remittance made yesterday?
→他們收到你昨天的匯款了嗎？

② **earnest** adj. 誠摯的、誠心的
If you have to do it, do it in an earnest way.
→要做的話，就真心去做。

③ **wonder** v. 猜想、納悶
I wonder if the rain will stop tomorrow.
→我在想明天雨會不會停。

④ **completely** adv. 完全地、徹底地
You completely let me down. →你徹底地讓我失望。

Unit 12 投訴違反合約

投訴對方**違反合約**條件時，該怎麼寫呢？ — □ ✕

Dear Mr. White,

I'm very disappointed to find that you have not settled the accounts for the order. According to the contract we signed, you should pay for the order in 5 months. We sincerely hope your company can deal with this matter soon. Please do follow the contract; otherwise, you will have to bear the consequence.

Beat wishes,

John Smith

親愛的懷特先生：

您尚未結算此次訂單的貨款，實在令人相當失望。按照雙方所簽署的合約，您應當在五個月內結算貨款。我們真誠希望貴公司能盡快處理此事。請遵守合約，否則後果自負。

真誠地，

約翰‧史密斯

Dear Mr. Smith,

We apologize for the failure to settle the accounts for the order. As the trucks are not sold out yet, we have some difficulties in fund **turnover**. Please accept our sincere apologies and we will make the payment as soon as possible. We assure you that you will receive the payment on time next time.

Yours sincerely,

Mike White

親愛的史密斯先生：

對於此次沒有準時支付貨款，我們深表歉意。因為我們的卡車尚未售完，所以我們在資金週轉方面有一些困難。請接受我們誠摯的道歉，我們會儘快支付此次貨款，並且保證下次準時支付。

真誠地，

麥克‧懷特

Dear Mr. Smith,

Thank you for your e-mail.

With reference to our letter on 5th, 9th, 17th of July, 2020, in which we made a **claim** on the quality of this order, your company did not take any **positive** action which would help clear the situation for us. According to the contract we signed before, we can **refuse** to pay for the order until you help to solve all the quality problems.

Sincerely hope you can understand it.

We look forward to having your early reply.

Chapter
1

Part 1
Part 2
Part 3

疑難雜症 Common situations

Part 4
Part 5
Part 6
Part 7

Best regards

Mike White

懷特先生：

您好！感謝您的回信。

在2020年7月5日、9日、以及17日的信中，我們已經告知此次貨物有品質問題。但是，貴公司沒有積極採取任何措施解決問題。根據我們之前簽署的合約，我們可以拒絕支付貨款，直到貴公司解決了所有的品質問題。希望您能理解。

希冀儘早回覆！

真誠地，

麥克・懷特

重點單字 記起來，寫信回信超精準

① **turnover** n. 流動、成交量、翻轉
The new product which has a fast turnover has been regarded as miracle. →擁有高成交量的新產品被視為是一項奇蹟。

② **claim** n./v. 要求、主張
What claim do you have to make such a request?
→你有何權利做此要求？

③ **positive** adj. 正向的、正面的
Look at the positive side: at least you didn't get fired.
→往好處想：至少你沒被解雇。

④ **refuse** v. 拒絕、不肯
I refuse to accept this offer. →我拒絕接受此提議。

Unit 13 | 售後服務投訴

想要投訴**售後服務**時，該怎麼寫呢？

Dear Sir / Madam,

As a customer who bought a laptop of your **brand** in October this year, I'm afraid I have to complain about your poor after-sales service.

I bought my laptop on 15th of October. In the first week, I could work for 3 hours with its **in-built** battery. However, after the first week, it can only last for less than 30 minutes, which greatly affects my work efficiency.

For this problem, I have contacted your after-sales service persons and requested door-to-door service. They told me that they would come to help me in three days. But now, one week has passed and no service persons came.

I'm telling you this problem in the hope that you can take real actions to solve the problem. Your quick response is highly appreciated.

Yours,

Joey

親愛的先生／女士：

我於今年10月份購買貴品牌的筆記型電腦。現在我要投訴你們的售後服務。

我於10月15日購買這台電腦。第一週，用電腦的內建電池我可以連續工作3小時。一週之後，這個電池連半小時都撐不了，這嚴重影響了我的工作效率。

Chapter

1

Part 1

Part 2

Part 3

疑難雜症 Common situations

Part 4

Part 5

Part 6

Part 7

關於這個問題,我聯繫了你們的售後服務人員,要求上門維修服務。他們告訴我,三天之內會來幫我檢查問題。現在已經一週了,還沒看到任何一個服務人員來查看。

告訴你這個問題是希望你能採取實際的措施來解決這個問題。希望您能儘快回覆。

真誠地,

喬伊

收到投訴**售後服務**的信時,該怎麼回呢? ─ □ ✕

Dear Joey,

We are sorry for the problem and inconvenience.

Currently, our after-sales service officer is checking this problem with service persons. I'm sure that they will find out the cause soon and give you a satisfactory reply.

Please accept our **heartfelt** apologies. We will contact you once we find a solution to the problem you mentioned. Thanks.

Best regards,
Lucy

親愛的喬伊:

很抱歉為您帶來麻煩和不便。

目前我們的售後服務部門正在與服務人員檢查問題。相信很快就能查明原因,並給您一個滿意的答覆。

我們表示誠摯的歉意。一旦找出解決上述問題的辦法,我們會立即與您聯繫。謝謝。

真誠地,
露西

不同的答覆還可以怎麼回呢？　　　— □ ✕

Dear Joey,

We are really sorry for the problem and all the inconvenience.

I have communicated with after-sales service department and they are **verifying** your problem. I will contact you once they work out the problem.

Please feel free to contact us if you have any other problem.

Yours Sincerely,
Lucy

親愛的喬伊：

很抱歉為您帶來問題和麻煩。

我已經與售後服務部門工作人員聯繫過，他們正在查明您所說的問題。一旦他們查明問題的原因，我會立即聯繫你。

如果您有任何其他問題，請隨時聯繫我們。

真誠地，
露西

重點單字記起來，寫信回信超精準

① **in-built** adj. 內建的
The in-built battery can only be purchased in America.
→此內建電池只能在美國買到。

② **heartfelt** adj. 衷心的、誠摯的
We received a heartfelt welcome by the hosts.
→我們受到主人誠摯的歡迎。

③ **verify** v. 證明、核對
Please provide relevant documents for us to verify the evidence. →請提供相關文件以便我們查核證據。

Unit 14 | 商品品質不佳

購買商品的**品質不佳**時，該怎麼寫呢？   — □ ✕

Dear Sir or Madam,

This letter is written in reference to your expensive Guess Watch I purchased from Parkson, a big department store of this town, on 15th of October. Unfortunately, the watch does not work after I bought it. I am very disappointed with my purchase.

On the advice of Parkson's manager, I am returning the watch to you.

Please make relevant arrangement for the watch to be fixed or replace it with a new one and send it to me as soon as possible.

Sincerely yours,

Abby

親愛的先生／女士：

本人於10月5日在本市的帕克森百貨公司購買了你們的Guess名錶一隻。遺憾的是，錶一拿回家就停了。我對所購買的商品非常失望。

按照帕克森百貨公司經理的建議，我把這支錶退還給你們。

請安排將錶修理好，或換一隻新的給我，並盼能早日寄來。

誠摯地，

艾比

Dear Sir,

Thank you for your letter on of 15th of October informing us the problem with your purchase and enclosing the defective Guess watch. We extremely regret that the watch you bought has caused you trouble.

We have passed your watch to our quality control department for **inspection** and report. Meanwhile, we are now making arrangement to send you a new one.

Please accept our apologies for the inconvenience.

Yours,
Parkson PR
Alice Wu

敬啟者：

您10月5日寄來的信及所附的故障Guess名錶已收到。您購買的Guess名錶給您造成麻煩，我們對此深感遺憾。

我們已將您的Guess名錶送交品質檢查部門檢驗，並要求做出報告。與此同時，我們正安排為您寄出新的錶。

對此事給您造成的不便深表歉意。

真誠地，
帕克森公關
愛麗絲吳

不同的答覆還可以怎麼回呢？   — □ ✕

Dear Abby,

Please accept our apologies for your purchase of a defective Guess Watch. By the time you read this, a new Guess watch has been arranged to be delivered to you.

Chapter

1

Part 1
Part 2
Part 3

疑難雜症 Common situations

Part 4
Part 5
Part 6
Part 7

Regarding this incident, I assure you that you can fully **rely on** our high-quality **luxury** watch. We are enclosing a gift as a small **gesture** to compensate for troubles and annoyance suffered on your side.

Yours truly,

Smith

Manager

親愛的艾比：

您10月15日購買的Guess名錶是一件瑕疵品，我們深表歉意。在你閱讀這封信函時，我們已經安排將一隻新錶寄送給您。

對此事件，我們向您保證，您可以完全相信我們高檔名錶的品質。我們隨信寄給您一件小禮物作為對此給您帶來的不便所作的小小補償。

經理
史密斯

重點單字 記起來，寫信回信超精準

① **inspection** n. 視察、監視、審查
The director was sent to the factory for product inspections. →處長被派去工廠做產品視察。

② **rely on** ph. 仰賴、依靠
I don't want to rely on my parents for financial support.
→我不想仰賴我父母的金援。

③ **luxury** n. 奢侈品、奢華、奢侈
What do you need all these luxuries for?
→你需要這麼多奢侈品做什麼？

④ **gesture** n. 姿勢、手勢示意 v. （以手）示意
The kiss was a warm gesture of farewell.
→那次親吻是道別的溫暖示意。

Unit 01 | 公司開業通知

要宣佈公司開設新店面的**開業通知**時，該怎麼寫呢？ ─ □ ✕

Dear Customers,

We are pleased to inform you that because of your support, our business grows very fast. Therefore, we have decided to open another store in Zhongshan Street on 1st of October, 2020.

In the new store, we will continue to provide you with high-quality clothing and **thoughtful** service.

Sincerely looking forward to your visit.

Yours faithfully,

James Brown

親愛的顧客：

我們很高興通知大家，由於您的支持，我們公司成長快速，因此，我們已經決定將於2020年10月1日在中山路開設一家新店。

在這家新店裡，我們將持續為您提供高品質服飾和貼心服務。

真心期待您的蒞臨。

誠摯地，

詹姆斯・布朗

Chapter

1

Part 1
Part 2
Part 3
Part 4

發布通知 Notifications

Part 5
Part 6
Part 7

身為顧客**收到開業通知信**時，該怎麼回呢？ — □ ✕

Dear Manager,

Congratulations to the opening of the new store.

I've been purchasing your clothes for 30 years. Your **delicate** style and comfortable design make me a fan of your clothes.

Wish your business **flourish**.

Yours ever,
Lisa Hunt

親愛的經理：

祝賀新店開張。

30年來我一直在你們店買衣服穿，你們衣服具有精緻的造型和舒服的設計使我成為忠誠顧客。

祝生意興隆。

真誠地，
麗莎・亨特

不同的答覆還可以怎麼回呢？ — □ ✕

Dear Manager,

I'm a **regular** guest in your store and I'm glad I have one more spot to do my shopping. Now I wonder if you're going to have any promotion events these days?

Yours,

Lisa Hunt

親愛的經理：

我是你們店的常客，很高興我現在又多了一個地方可以購物。我想知道在新店開張期間你們有沒有任何促銷活動？

真誠地，

麗莎·亨特

 重點單字記起來，寫信回信超精準

① **thoughtful** adj. 體貼的、考慮周到的
Your thoughtful plans have earned the Board's approval. →你思慮周到的計畫已經贏得董事會的贊同。

② **delicate** adj. 柔和的、精美的、雅致的、纖弱的
This kind of rose is rather delicate and withers quickly. →這種玫瑰相當脆弱且很快就會凋謝了。

③ **flourish** v. 繁榮、興旺、茂盛、活躍
The Asia market is flouring and we should introduce our product ASAP.
→亞洲市場正繁榮，我們應盡快引進我們的產品。

④ **regular** adj. 規律的、規則的、定期的
She has no regular jobs and hence the irregular income. →她沒有固定工作，所以收入也不固定。

Unit 02 | 暫停營業通知

要宣佈**暫停營業**時，該怎麼寫呢？

Dear Customers,

We are writing this letter to inform you that Dia Supermarket in Dongjun street will be closed **temporarily** from October 18 to 30 due to **renovations**.

We are going to reopen on the 1st of November. Please accept our apologies for any inconvenience it may cause you.

We sincerely expect your visit in the future.

Best wishes,

Julia Peterson

親愛的顧客朋友：

您好！此信是想通知您，由於東峻大街的迪亞超市將重新裝修，所以10月18日至30日這段期間我們將暫停營業。

我們將於11月1日重新開張。對於此次裝修暫停營業可能給您帶來的任何不便，敬請見諒。

真誠期待您日後來訪。

祝福您，

茱麗亞・彼得森

收到**暫停營業**的信，該怎麼回呢？　　　　　　　— □ ✕

Dear manager,

Got it. But could you please send us a list with the address of other Dia stores? I spent much time finding another one yesterday.

Yours sincerely,

Aster Dong

親愛的經理：

瞭解。但不知您能否給我們一份迪亞其他分店的地址？昨天我找了好久才找到另一家。

誠摯地，

艾斯特・董

不同的答覆還可以怎麼回呢？　　　　　　　— □ ✕

Dear manager,

Actually, I want to **complain** about the **construction**. I've been woken up for due to the noise in the middle of the night for almost 2 weeks.

Maybe you can finish the renovations faster, or at least start after 8:30 am?

Hope it won't trouble you.

Sincerely,

Aster Dong

親愛的經理：

事實上我想投訴你們整修的事。我幾乎有兩個禮拜的時間都被你們的凌晨的噪音吵醒。

Chapter
1

Part 1
Part 2
Part 3
Part 4

發布通知 Notifications

Part 5
Part 6
Part 7

也許你們可以盡快完成裝修工程，或者至少在早上8:30以後開工？

希望不會令你太為難。

誠摯地，

艾斯特・董

 重點單字記起來，寫信回信超精準

① **temporarily** adv. 暫時地
The branch office in Taichung was temporarily closed due to the pandemic. →因流行性疾病影響，台中分公司暫時關閉。

② **renovation** n. 修理、整修
The living room needs some renovations. What's our budget? →客廳需要整修了，我們的預算有多少？

③ **complain** v. 發牢騷、抱怨、控訴
My sister kept complaining about her long working hours. →我姐姐一直抱怨她的工時很長。

④ **construction** n. 建造、建築物
The mansion under construction is predicted to be finished by 2025.
→那棟正在建造中的豪宅預計2025 年竣工。

Unit 03 | 更改營業時間

需要宣佈**更改營業時間**時，該怎麼寫呢？ ─ □ ✕

Dear Customers,

We are pleased to announce that our new business hours will be from 8:00 a.m. to 10:30 p.m., Monday to Friday since 1st of June, 2020. We sincerely hope that this change of working hours will bring you more convenience on your shopping.

We promise we will provide the most efficient and **heartfelt** service for you as we always do.

Yours faithfully,

New World Shopping Mall

親愛的顧客朋友：

我們很高興在這宣佈，從2020年6月1日開始，我們的營業時間將變更為每週一到週五的上午八點至晚上十點半。我們真誠的希望透過變更營業時間，能為您的購物帶來更多的便利。

我保證我們會一如既往的給大家帶來最佳的效率和真心的服務。

誠摯地，

新世界購物中心

Chapter

1

Part 1
Part 2
Part 3
Part 4

發布通知 Notifications

Part 5
Part 6
Part 7

收到**更改營業時間**的信時，該怎麼回呢？ — □ ✕

To whom it might concern,

We're glad you make this adjustment. The new business hours truly **benefit** most of us since your target basically work nine to five.

Yours ever,

Jen

致相關人士：

很高興你們做了此調整。新的營業時間真的對我們來說有所助益，畢竟你的目標客群大多都是朝九晚五的上班族。

真誠地，

珍

不同的答覆還可以怎麼回呢？ — □ ✕

To whom it might concern,

It surprises me that you **adopted** my suggestion!

So, to **repay** my good piece of advice, how about sending me a discount card?

Yours ever,

Jen

致相關人士：

你們採納了我的建議，真令我訝異！

因此，為了回報我的好建議，送我一張折扣卡如何？

誠摯地，

珍

重點單字記起來，寫信回信超精準

① **heartfelt** `adj.` 衷心的、誠摯的
Please accept our heartfelt apologies for the mistake.
→請接受我們對錯誤真心誠意的道歉。

② **benefit** `v.` 有益於、受惠 `n.` 益處、好處
I'm sure this policy will benefit all personnel in the company. →我相信此政策會給公司所有員工帶來好處。

③ **adopt** `v.` 採用、採納、收養
The manager decided to adopt our proposal for the new advertisement. →經理決定採用我們對新廣告的提案。

④ **repay** `v.` 付還、回報、報復
She'll repay the money she owned you tomorrow.
→她明天會還你她向你借的錢。

Unit 04 | 公司搬遷通知

要宣佈**公司搬遷通知**時，確認信該怎麼寫呢？ — □ ✕

Dear Customers,

We are pleased to announce that our company will be moved to Room 308, E Building, Oriental Plaza on 15 of March, 2020. Our postal address will be changed to #1 Wangfujing Street, but our contact number **remains** unchanged.

All staffs from our company take this **opportunity** to thank you for your support and attention.

Yours faithfully,

Ron Edgar

EGO Company

親愛的客戶：

很高興在這裡宣佈，本公司自2020年3月15日起將遷至東方廣場E棟308室。我們的郵寄的址改為：王府井大街1號，東方廣場E棟308室。我們的聯絡電話保持不變。

本公司全體員工藉此機會感謝您對我們的支持與關注。

誠摯的

朗・艾德格

EGO公司

Dear Mr. Edgar,

Announcement received. We will update it to our contact list.

Wish your business flourish.

Sincerely yours,
Rose Hill

親愛的艾德格先生：

已經收到你們的通知了，我們將會更新公司的聯絡表。

祝生意興隆。

誠摯地，
羅斯・希爾

Dear Mr. Edgar,

Thanks for your notice. New place, new start. I believe you can have a nice **performance** this year.

Let's keep in touch as always.

Sincerely yours,
Rose Hill

親愛的艾德格先生：

感謝您的通知。

新的環境代表新的開始，相信你們今年一定有很好的表現。

像往常一樣保持聯繫。

誠摯地，
羅斯・希爾

Chapter
1

Part 1
Part 2
Part 3
Part 4

發布通知 Notifications

Part 5
Part 6
Part 7

重點單字記起來，寫信回信超精準

① **remain** v. 剩下、餘留、保持、仍是
Several homeless men remained on the street after the parade. →遊行後街上有幾個流浪漢徘徊著。

② **opportunity** n. 機會
Grab the opportunity, or else you may never get promoted in the future. →把握機會，才不會在未來就無法升遷了。

③ **announcement** n. 公告、宣告
The government made the announcement that gathering over 20 people are banned.

→政府公告超過20人以上的集會都將禁止。

④ **performance** n. 性能、表演、執行、績效
How's the performance of this avant-garde gadget?

→這個新潮的器具性能怎樣？

Unit 05 | 暫時停業通知

要宣佈**公司停業**時,該怎麼寫呢? ─ □ ✕

Dear Sirs,

This is to notify you our working schedule during National Day.

According to government regulations, our office will be closed on Friday, 1st of October, 2020 till 7 of October, 2020.

We would also like to take this opportunity to thank you for your support and we wish you a happy holiday!

Best regards,

Star **Advertising** Co, Ltd.

親愛的客戶:

我們藉此機會通知您本公司在國慶日期間的日程安排。

根據政府規定,我們將於2020年10月1日至2020年10月7日休假。

我們也想藉此機會感謝您對我們的支持,並祝各位度過一個愉快的假期!

真誠地,

思達廣告有限公司

Chapter

1

Part 1
Part 2
Part 3

Part 4

發布通知 Notifications

Part 5
Part 6
Part 7

收到**暫時停業**的信時，該怎麼回呢？   — □ ✕

Dear Sir,

Thanks for the notification. We will arrange our work to **avoid** any possible delaying.

Have a nice **holiday**!

Best regards,
FJ PR Company

....

各位：

感謝通知。我們會安排好工作，以避免任何可能延遲的機會。

祝假期愉快！

真誠地，
FJ公關公司

不同的答覆還可以怎麼回呢？   — □ ✕

Dear Sir,

We are preparing an urgent paperwork for our **mutual** client-NHT now and might need your help during the holiday. We'll greatly appreciate if you can help on that.

Best regards,
FJ PR Company

....

各位：

我們正為我們共同的客戶-NHT準備一份緊急檔案，也許在休假期間需要你們的協助。如果能得到你們的幫助，我們將會非常感激。

真誠地，
FJ公關公司

 **重點單字**記起來，寫信回信超精準

① **advertising** n. 廣告業、做廣告、登廣告、廣告
His marketing techniques are well-known in the advertising industry. →他的行銷手法在廣告界很知名。

② **avoid** v. 避免、避開、躲避
Such careless mistake should be avoided by all means. →這種無心錯誤應全力避免。

③ **holiday** n. 假期、節日、假日
I hate working on holidays with no overtime pay!
→我討厭假日無償上班！

④ **mutual** adj. 相互的、彼此的、共同的
A healthy relationship relies on mutual respect.
→一段健康的關係仰賴共同尊重。

Unit 06 | 求職錄用通知

要通知面試者**錄取結果**時，該怎麼寫呢？

Dear Miss Molly Wang,

It is a great pleasure to inform you that we have decided to hire you as our Personal **Assistant** to General Manager, **effective** on 1st of July, 2020.

We will send you an **offer** letter within three working days. Please do not hesitate to call us if you have any questions.

We are looking forward to your coming!

Yours sincerely,

Sunshine International Trade Company

親愛的王茉莉小姐：

非常高興的通知您，我們已經決定自2020年7月1日起錄用你為本公司總經理助理。我們會在三個工作日內將聘書寄給您。如果您還有任何問題，盡請與我們聯繫。

期待您的加入！

誠摯地，

陽光國際貿易公司

Dear HR,

Thanks for your kindly notification. It's my pleasure to be a part of you, and I'll **dedicate** myself to this company.

I am looking forward to the offer letter.

Sincerely yours,
Molly Wang

親愛的人事部：

謝謝你們的通知，能進入貴公司工作是我的榮幸，我會全身心投入到工作中。

期待你們的聘書。

真誠地，
王茉莉

不同的答覆還可以怎麼回呢？ — □ ×

Dear Manager,

I'd like to thank you for choosing me as your assistant. I'll work hard in the future and try my best to offer you help on business.

Sincerely yours,
Molly Wang

親愛的經理：

感謝您選擇我作為您的助理。今後我會努力工作，盡力為您提供工作上的幫助。

真誠地，
王茉莉

Chapter
1

Part 1
Part 2
Part 3
Part 4

發布通知 Notifications

Part 5
Part 6
Part 7

重點單字記起來，寫信回信超精準

① **assistant** n. 助理、助手
She was hired as an assistant to the Dean of the Academic Affairs. →她被聘為學務處長的助理。

② **effective** adj. 有效的、有用的、生效的
The bill will become effective after the President gives her consent. →在總統同意之後此法案立即生效。

③ **offer** n. 提供、出價、工作機會 v. 給予、提議
I'm sorry that I have to decline this offer since I still on holidays. →因尚在休假，很抱歉我必須拒絕此工作機會。

④ **dedicate** v. 貢獻、供奉
My father dedicated his life to the research of astronomy. →我爸爸貢獻其一生研究天文學。

Unit 07 人員裁減通知

要宣佈**裁員**時，該怎麼寫呢？

Dear Victoria,

As you might have been aware, we are having a very difficult time of corporation **reorganization**. We have tried our best to keep all of our hardworking staff. Unfortunately, it is regretful that we have to inform you a piece of bad news. We can no longer keep you in our company anymore.

We are grateful for your work during your **tenure** of employment and we feel very sorry to lose you.

We wish you a bright future!

Yours truly,
HR Department
EGO Co.

親愛的維多莉雅：

可能你也能夠瞭解，本公司正處於重組的艱困期。 我們盡可能的保留住公司內的全體員工。但遺憾的是，我們不得不告訴您一個壞消息，您將被解除職位。

我們一直都對您在就職期間的表現很滿意。我們為失去您的效力感到非常遺憾。

祝福您有更好的發展！

真誠地，

EGO公司人力資源部

Chapter
1

Part 1
Part 2
Part 3
Part 4

發布通知 Notifications

Part 5
Part 6
Part 7

回覆公司的**裁員信**時，該怎麼寫呢？　— □ ✕

Dear all,

I'm sorry that I can't serve in this company any longer. I've learned and gained so much in this great company.

I feel sad to part from you, but we can always cooperate in the future.

Wish you all the best.
Yours ever,
Victoria

親愛的大家：

非常遺憾不能繼續為公司服務。我在這裡學到以及獲得了許多東西。

離開你們是件傷心的事，但只要我們願意，未來總可以合作。

真誠地，
維多莉雅

不同的答覆還可以怎麼回呢？　— □ ✕

Dear HR,

I wonder the reason for which I have to leave.

I've been working in this company since it was established 4 years ago, and I've been hard working all the time. I **acquired** an important client and was The Best Seller last year. So, my question is why I am the person who's going to be kicked out?

I don't mean to **offend** but just want to get a reasonable explanation.

Victoria

親愛的人事部：

我想知道我被裁員的原因。

我在這間公司4年前創立之始就在這裡工作，一直以來都非常努力。去年我獲得了一位重要的客戶，還獲得了「最佳銷售員」的榮譽，所以我的問題是，為什麼被裁掉的是我？

我無意冒犯，只是希望得到一個合理的解釋。

真誠地，

維多莉雅

重點單字記起來，寫信回信超精準

① **reorganization** n. 整頓、改編、重新制定
The reorganization of the Literature Department was deemed as a failure. →文學系的改組工作被認為是場失敗。

② **tenure** n. 任期、佔有
The refusal of the tenure was rather a great shock to him. →被拒絕終身職對他來說相當是個衝擊。

③ **acquire** v. 獲得、學到、取得、捕獲
I finally acquired the degree after years of hard work.
→在多年的勤奮付出之後，我終於拿到了學位。

④ **offend** v. 冒犯、觸怒
His ignorance not only offended her but deeply hurt her feelings. →他的無知不僅觸犯到她，也深深地傷害了她的情感。

Unit 08｜人事變動通知

Dear all the staff,

I am very pleased to announce the **appointment** of Ms. Alice Jackson as the director of Accounting Department of Future Company. Alice **possesses** 12 years of experience in accounting and her **extensive** knowledge and experience will be an **invaluable** asset to our company.

Please join us in welcoming Alice to Future Company!

Sincerely yours,

John Smith

親愛的同事們：

我非常高興的宣佈，愛麗絲‧傑克森將擔任未來公司的財務部門總監一職。愛麗絲女士在財務工作方面擁有長達12年的工作經驗，並且她淵博的知識和閱歷將會是本公司不可估量的資產。

請大家一起歡迎愛麗絲加入公司！

約翰‧史密斯

Dear Mr. Smith,

We are looking forward to Alice's coming and have prepared a welcome party for her.

We'd like to invite you to join us on Saturday evening. Hope you're available that time.

Sincerely yours,

Frank Gao

親愛的史密斯先生：

我們期待愛麗絲的到來，準備為她舉辦一個歡迎會。

我們也誠摯邀請您參加週六晚上的歡迎會，希望到時您有空參加。

誠摯地，

法蘭克・高

Dear Mr. Smith,

We're glad to have a new director for the Accounting Department. We've been looking forward to this famous director for a long time.

Believe we can get better under her leadership.

Sincerely yours,

Frank Gao

親愛的史密斯先生：

我們很高興將有一位新的財務總監。我們期待這位業內的名人很久了。

Chapter

1

Part 1

Part 2

Part 3

Part 4

發布通知 Notifications

Part 5

Part 6

Part 7

相信在她的管理下我們公司能越來越好。

法蘭克・高

重點單字記起來，寫信回信超精準

① **appointment** n. 任命、約定、任命的職位、約會
I have an appointment with my dentist this afternoon.
→我今天下午要去看牙醫。

② **possess** v. 擁有、持有、獲得
Adam is possessed of great patience and wisdom.
→亞當是個擁有極佳耐心和智慧的人。

③ **extensive** adj. 廣泛的、廣闊的、大量的
Extensive reading is crucial to the acquirement of a language. →廣泛閱讀對語言習得來說非常關鍵。

④ **invaluable** adj. 無價的、非常貴重的
All my loved ones are invaluable for me and no one can replace them.
→我所愛之人對我來說是無價的，且無人能取代。

Unit 01 | 邀請參加宴會

想邀請對方**參與宴會**時，該怎麼寫呢？

Dear Mr. Murphy,

We are pleased to invite you and your wife to attend our celebration dinner for the 50th **anniversary** of our company. The dinner will be held from 19:00 to 21:00 at Crystal Palace in Hilton Hotel on 20 of Oct., 2020.

It is a **formal** dinner. Please confirm with us if you would like to join the celebration by Thursday. Thanks.

Looking forward to your and your wife's **attendance**.

Yours sincerely,

Ben Affleck

親愛的墨菲先生：

我們非常榮幸地邀請您及尊夫人參加我們公司成立50週年的慶祝晚宴。本次晚宴將在2020年10月20日晚間19點至21點在希爾頓飯店的水晶宮舉行。

此為正式晚宴。請您與本週四前和我們確認您們是否參加晚宴。謝謝。

期待著您與貴夫人的光臨。

真誠地，

班‧艾佛列克

Chapter

1

Part 1
Part 2
Part 3
Part 4
Part 5

社交邀請 Social invitations

Part 6
Part 7

收到**宴會邀請**的信，該怎麼回呢？　　　— ☐ ✕

Dear Mr. Affleck,

It's our pleasure to receive the invitation. My wife and I will be there on time.

Happy anniversary to this great company in advance.

Sincerely yours,

Murphy

親愛的艾佛列克先生：

能被邀請是我們的榮幸。我和妻子將準時赴宴。

提前祝這間偉大的公司生日快樂。

真誠地，

墨菲

不同的答覆還可以怎麼回呢？　　　— ☐ ✕

Dear Mr. Affleck,

It's kind of you to invite us, but I have to apologize for my future **absence**. I'll be in Japan for business reasons at that time.

My apologies in advance. Have a wonderful celebration.

Sincerely yours,

Murphy

親愛的艾佛列克先生：

您邀請我們是我們的榮幸，但非常抱歉我無法參加。那個時間我將在日本處理一些工作上的事務。

我預先道歉。希望你們擁有一個精彩的慶祝晚宴。

真誠地，

墨菲

重點單字記起來，寫信回信超精準

① **anniversary** n. 週年紀念
This Sunday is my parent's 30th anniversary.
→這週日是我爸媽的結婚三十週年紀念日。

② **formal** adj. 正式的、形式上的
You should wear a formal dress to a formal banquet.
→你應著正式裙裝參加正式宴會。

③ **attendance** n. 出席、到場
Punctual attendance in this class is mandatory.
→準時出席在這堂課是必須的。

④ **absence** n. 缺席、缺乏
The absence of our CEO rendered the meeting pointless.
→總裁缺席讓這場會議毫無意義。

Unit 02 | 邀請參與訪談

想邀請對方**參與訪談**時，該怎麼寫呢？　　　　

Dear Professor Lee,

I am very delighted to invite you as a **visiting scholar** in Taiwan. You will stay at National Taiwan University during your visit. As a visiting scholar, you can pursue your study on economic development and communicate with the National Taiwan University **faculty** during your stay.

If you have any further inquiries regarding this matter, please be free to call us. We are looking forward to your visit.

Yours sincerely,
Dakota Johnson
Dean of Economics Department
National Taiwan University

親愛的李教授：

您好！我們高興地邀請您作為訪問學者來台灣參觀訪問。你來訪期間，國立台灣大學將負責接待您。訪問期間，您也可以進行經濟發展研究，並訪問其他大學，並與雪梨大學的在校師生進行交流合作。學者可隨心所欲的交流。

如就此事您有任何疑問，敬請告知我們。我們期待您的到訪。

真誠地，
達科塔・強森
國立台灣大學經濟系主任

收到邀請**參加訪談**的信時，該怎麼回呢？　－ □ ✕

Dear Professor Johnson,

It's my great honor to receive your invitation.

National Taiwan University is one of the greatest universities in the world, and I'm glad I am **granted** a chance to a visiting scholar of it.

Will prepare for this matter.

Regards,

Lee Hua

親愛的強森教授：

收到您的邀請是我極大的榮幸。

國立台灣大學是世界上最好的大學之一，我非常高興能作為它的訪問學者。

將積極準備具體事宜。

誠摯地，

李華

不同的答覆還可以怎麼回呢？　－ □ ✕

Dear Professor Johnson,

Thanks for inviting me to be a visiting scholar of National Taiwan University. I plan to go to Sydney in summer next year. Before that, I have to prepare for several application materials for my overseas studies.

We can have afternoon coffee together next summer if everything goes smoothly.

Regards,

Lee Hua

Chapter

1

Part 1
Part 2
Part 3
Part 4
Part 5
社交邀請 Social invitations
Part 6
Part 7

尊敬的強森教授：

感謝您邀請我做國立台灣大學的訪問學者。我計畫在明年夏天去雪梨。在那之前，我得替我的海外研究準備許多申請資料。

如果一切順利的話，下個夏天來臨的時候我們就能一起喝咖啡了。

再次感謝並致敬，

張華

 **重點單字**記起來，寫信回信超精準

① **visiting** adj. 參觀的、訪問的
I have the visiting rights to my children.
→我有對我孩子的探訪權。

② **scholar** n. 學者
Mr. Barry is a prestigious and conscientious scholar.
→拜瑞先生是名具有聲望與良知的學者。

③ **faculty** n. 全體教職員
Welcome to join the faculty of our beloved Sunflower University! →歡迎加入太陽花大學這個大家庭！

④ **grant** v. 同意、准予、授與
His company granted him only a small pension.
→他的公司只給他以小筆退休金。

Unit 03 | 研討會議與會

邀請**參加研討會**時，該怎麼寫呢？

Dear Mr. Landes,

It is my pleasure to invite you to attend the conference regarding the **economic** growth in the Asia-Pacific **region** in Hong Kong on 23 of July, 2020. All of your travel expense will be **subsidized**. If you are interested in this conference, please let us know by next Thursday, 3rd of June, 2020.

Please find the attached detail introduction about this conference.

I am looking forward to your early reply.

Sincerely yours,

Alexia Anderson

親愛的藍迪斯先生：

我非常榮幸的邀請您出席2020年7月23日在香港舉辦的亞太經濟發展研討會。您所有的差旅費用都將由我們支付。如您有意參加，請於2020年6月3日，下週四之前和我們確認。

請查收附件為本次會議的詳細介紹。

期待您的儘早回覆。

真誠地，

艾莉西雅・安德森

Chapter
1

Part 1
Part 2
Part 3
Part 4
Part 5

社交邀請 Social invitations

Part 6
Part 7

收到**研討會議邀請**時，該怎麼回呢？   — □ ✕

Dear Madam,

I'm interested in this topic; unfortunately, I will be in Mexico for another international conference at that time.

It's a pity that I cannot attend the event with you. May you have a successful conference.

Regards,

Beck Landes

....

女士：

我對這個議題很感興趣，不幸的是，那個時間我將在墨西哥參加另一個國際會議。

不能參加你們的活動我很遺憾。預祝大會圓滿成功。

致敬，
貝克・藍迪斯

不同的答覆還可以怎麼回呢？   — □ ✕

Dear Madam,

I feel honorable to be a part of this conference. I will prepare a speech on the conference to share with people my new **viewpoints** on the issue.

Regards,

Beck Landes

....

女士：

能參加這次會議我感到很榮幸。我會準備一個演講在會議上發言，和大家分享我的新觀點。

致敬，
貝克・藍迪斯

重點單字記起來，寫信回信超精準

① **economic** adj. 經濟的、經濟學的
From an economic regard, this plan is downright infeasible. →從經濟的層面來看，這個計畫完全不可行。

② **region** n. 區域、領域、地區
The North is a rather cold region, but famous for skiing. →北方是相當冷的區域，但是滑雪很出名。

③ **subsidize** v. 給予津貼、補助
Many industries are subsidized by the government right now. →現在許多產業皆接受政府補助。

④ **viewpoint** n. 觀點、視角
I'd like to know more about your viewpoint on this issue. →我想多知道你對此議題的觀點。

Unit 04 | 參與新聞發佈

邀請對方參加**新聞發佈會**時，該怎麼寫呢？ — □ ✕

Dear Sirs,

The **investigation** on the **polluted** river nearby Tianyi Natural Beauty Area has been closed. The report of the investigation will be announced at 14:00-15:30 on 17 of November, 2020, in Daisy Garden conference room in Full-link Building. The press conference will be held by Taiwan Environment Protection Association (CEPA).

To **facilitate** your background knowledge about the issue, please refer to the attached document.

We sincerely expect your attendance.

Yours faithfully,
Mandy Liu
Contact person from TEPA

敬啟者：

針對發生在天一自然風景區附近的河流污染事件調查已經結束。調查報告將於2020年11月17日下午2點到3點半在豐聯廣場的菊花園會議廳公佈。這個新聞發佈會將由台灣環境保護協會舉辦。

為了使您對此次事件的背景知識有更多瞭解，請閱讀附件檔。

我們真誠地期待各位的光臨。

真誠地，
曼蒂·劉
台灣環境保護協會會議聯繫人

Dear Ms. Liu,

I am a reporter from Times Asia magazine, and I am deeply concern about this investigation. I wonder if I can have an **exclusive** interview with you after the announcement. It will only take you about half an hour.

Best Regards,

Richard Jule

. . . .

親愛的劉先生：

我是《時代亞洲》雜誌的記者，非常關心這次調查。不知道在發佈會結束後能不能對您做一個專訪，只需耽誤您大約半小時。

真誠地，

理查・朱爾

Dear Mandy,

Thanks for your invitation. We'll be there on time.

Best Regards,

Richard Jule

. . . .

親愛的曼蒂：

謝謝你的邀請，我們會準時到達會場。

真誠地，

理查・朱爾

Chapter
1

Part 1
Part 2
Part 3
Part 4
Part 5
社交邀請 Social invitations
Part 6
Part 7

重點單字記起來，寫信回信超精準

① **investigation** n. 調查、研究
After thorough investigation, the factory is the perpetrator of the pollution.
→經過徹底的調查，該工廠是污染的罪魁禍首。

② **pollute** v. 污染、弄髒、玷污
Plastic products pollute our environment in many ways. →塑膠產品以不同方式污染著我們的環境。

③ **facilitate** v. 促進、使容易
The introduction of the new machine facilitates the speed of the production line.
→引進新產品幫助加速整個產品線的速度。

④ **exclusive** adj. 排外的、獨有的、專一的
The meal charges 200 NTD, exclusive of tips.
→這頓飯共200元，不含小費。

Unit 05 | 擔任發言角色

想邀請對方**擔任發言人**時，該怎麼寫呢？

Dear Ms. Zheng,

We would like to invite you to be our **spokesperson** for the Taipei Public Transportation **Summit** 2020. We believe that no one can fill this role better than you. Taipei Public Transportation Association (BJ PTA) will take care of all of your expenses. The media panel will begin at 10 a.m. on 14 of October, 2020 and it last **approximately** for two hours.

We sincerely hope you can **undertake** this position and please let me know if you can by 30 of September, 2020.

Looking forward to your response.

Yours faithfully,

Jennifer Yan
From BJ PTA

親愛的曾女士：

我們想邀請您擔任台北2020城市交通高峰會的發言人。我們認為沒有人比您更適合擔任這個角色了。台北城市交通協會將全額贊助您的支出。媒體討論會將於2020年10月14日上午十點開始，會議歷時約2小時。

我們衷心希望您能承接這個位置，並請您於2020年9月30日前把您的決定告知我們。期待著您的回覆。

真誠地，

珍妮佛・嚴
台北城市交通協會

Chapter

1

Part 1
Part 2
Part 3
Part 4
Part 5

社交邀請 Social invitations

Part 6
Part 7

收到**擔任發言人**的邀請信時，該怎麼回呢？ — ☐ ✕

Dear Jennifer,

I'm pleasant to take it because it's a meaningful event. I'll arrive in Taipei on 12 of Oct. and get myself ready for the Summit.

Yours truly,

Zheng Meng

親愛的珍妮佛：

我很愉快接受這份工作因為這是一次有意義的大會。我將在10月12日到達台北，為高峰會的召開做好準備。

誠摯地，

曾夢

不同的答覆還可以怎麼回呢？ — ☐ ✕

Dear Jennifer,

I'm so sorry that I can't accept the invitation this time because I'm not in a good health condition these days. I basically cannot do anything on my own and rely heavily on people around me just to move around.

But if you don't mind, I could recommend another person to take my part. Will you please call me when you get the email?

Yours truly,

Zheng Meng

親愛的珍妮佛：

我很抱歉不能接受你們的邀請，因為我最近身體狀況真的不太好，我基本上無法自行做事，需要仰賴他人活動。

如果你們不介意我可以推薦另一個人代替我的角色。收到郵件後能打個電話給我嗎？

誠摯地，

曾夢

重點單字 記起來，寫信回信超精準

① **spokesperson** n. 發言人
She used to be the spokesperson of that international corporation. →她曾是那間國際企業的發言人。

② **summit** n. 高峰、尖峰
All world leaders are predicted to attend the summit held in Lima. →世界領導人具預測皆將參與於利馬舉行的高峰會。

③ **approximately** adv. 大約地、大致上地
Approximately 300 people will participate in the championship. →大約 300 人會參與此次錦標賽。

④ **undertake** v. 承擔、保證、從事
The squad will undertake this dangerous secret mission. →小組將進行此次危險的秘密任務。

Unit 06 | 出席紀念活動

想要邀請對方出席紀念活動時，該怎麼寫呢？ ⚊ ☐ ✕

Dear Mr. Wang,

On 15th of May, the **Board** of our university plans to hold the 30th anniversary for our university, with a **celebratory** reception at our Yifu Building on Saturday, 15 of May between 14:00 and 18:00. Afterwards, there will be a dinner party.

We are very happy to invite you to join the ceremony and the dinner party. We would appreciate it if you could confirm with us about your **availability** before 10 of April.

Sincerely yours,

Mavis Fang

親愛的王先生：

我們學校董事會計畫在五月十五日舉行我們大學建校30週年的紀念日。下午兩點到晚上八點會在逸夫樓舉辦一個慶祝接待會，之後還會有一個晚宴。

我們非常高興地邀請您參加慶典和晚宴，並且如您能在四月十日之前和我們確認您能否與會，我們將不勝感激。

真誠地，

梅維斯・方

Dear Mavis,

Thanks for the invitation; I will be there on time.

And I'd like to **sponsor** the reception to express my gratitude to my mother school.

Yours sincerely,

Wang Hsin

親愛的梅維斯：

謝謝邀請，我一定準時參加。

並且，我想贊助這次的接待會，以表達我對母校的感激之情。

誠摯地，
王新

不同的答覆還可以怎麼回呢？   — □ ✕

Dear Mavis,

I'm afraid that I can't be there at that time. I'll be in another city and may not make it.

Anyhow, cheers for our mother school!

Yours sincerely,

Wang Hsin

親愛的梅維斯：

恐怕我沒辦法參加。我到時後會在另一個城市，可能無法趕達。不管怎樣，為我們的母校賀喜！

誠摯地，
王新

Chapter
1

Part 1
Part 2
Part 3
Part 4
Part 5
社交邀請 Social invitations
Part 6
Part 7

重點單字記起來，寫信回信超精準

① **board** n. 董事會、理事會
Joining the board of the corporation made him rejoice. →加入公司董事會令他開心。

② **celebratory** adj. 慶祝的、快樂的
Let's have a celebratory drink to the winning of the award! →讓我們為了獲獎喝慶功酒吧！

③ **availability** n. 可用性、有效性、可得性
When demand exceeds availability, inflation ensues.
→當供不應求，物價就會上漲。

④ **sponsor** v. 贊助、發起 n. 主辦人、贊助商
The championship failed to have enough sponsors and was hence canceled.
→錦標賽無法獲得足夠贊助，因此取消了。

Unit 07 | 邀請進行合作

想要邀請對方**一同合作**時，該怎麼寫呢？　

Dear Mr. Affleck,

I am greatly honored to invite you to work with our team on the project of B software development for the following six months in our company. I have already reached an agreement with a big client, and I am confident in our **output** in six months.

In addition to a **fairly** good pay, our company will also be very delighted to cover all your **expenses**, including **accommodation** and transportation costs, etc.

We expect to work with you.

Truly yours,

Will Smith

親愛的艾佛列克先生：

我非常榮幸的邀請您在未來的六個月加入本團隊共同完成B軟體的開發專案。我們已經和一個大客戶達成了合作協定，我對我們六個月之後的成果非常有信心。

除了一份豐厚的待遇，我們公司也會非常願意為您支付所有的費用，其中包括食宿費用及交通費用等。

我們期待與您合作。

真誠地，

威爾·史密斯

Chapter 1

Part 1
Part 2
Part 3
Part 4
Part 5
Part 6
Part 7

社交邀請 Social invitations

回覆對方**邀請合作**的信時，該怎麼寫呢？　─ □ ✕

Dear Will,

I accepted this generous collaboration invitation, and should arrive at your office within 3 hours. See you later.

Yours,

Affleck

親愛的威爾：

我答應你的慷慨邀請，並將在3小時之內到你那裡。晚點見。

誠摯地，

艾佛列克

不同的答覆還可以怎麼回呢？　─ □ ✕

Dear Will,

I'm very interested in the project and we've certainly had pleasant cooperation before. But now I'm engaged in another important project that has an urgent deadline to meet. Is it possible that the project you mentioned begin one week later?

Yours,

Affleck

親愛的威爾：

我對這專案十分感興趣，且我們有非常愉快的合作經驗，但我現在正在參與另一個重要的專案，快到截止日了。你能接受你提及的專案晚一個禮拜再開始嗎？

誠摯地，

艾佛列克

重點單字記起來，寫信回信超精準

① **output** n. 產出、產量
This machine can double the output for at least one year. →這台機器能使產能加倍至少一年。

② **fairly** adv. 頗為、相當地
She is a fairly decent scholar.
→她是一位相當正直的學者。

③ **expense** n. 支出、花費、開銷
Household expenses account for a great part of our income. →家庭支出佔了我們收入相當大的一部份。

④ **accommodation** n. 膳宿、住宿
Can you help us book overnight accommodations?
→你能幫我們訂過夜的住處嗎？

Unit 08 | 接受邀請信函

要回覆對方的**邀請信**時，該怎麼寫呢？　

Dear Mr. Li,

Thank you so much for inviting me to attend the 10th anniversary of your company at 7 p.m. on 28 of October, 2020 at Lotus Palace in Rainbow Hotel.

I am very pleased to accept your invitation. Look forward to seeing you at the event.

Sincerely yours,

Rose Guan

親愛的李先生：

感謝您熱情邀請我參加10月28日19時貴公司在彩虹飯店蓮花宮舉辦的10週年慶祝活動。

我很高興接受你的邀請。期待與您見面。

誠摯地，

羅斯・關

收到對方**接受邀請**的信時，該怎麼回呢？   — ▢ ✕

Dear Mr. Guan,

We're glad you accept our invitation. We'll make sure to make you **feel at home** at the venue.

Yours truly,

Li

親愛的關先生：

很高興您接受邀請。我們會竭盡所能讓您享受活動。

摯誠地，

李

不同的答覆還可以怎麼回呢？   — ▢ ✕

Dear Mr. Guan,

It's **fantastic** you can come. However, we have to make a **correction** that the anniversary will be held at 8 p.m., not 7 p.m. Please accept our apologies for making such a mistake. We know you'll have to **rearrange** your schedule. Sorry for any inconvenience caused.

Yours truly,

Li

親愛的關先生：

您能來真是太好了。但我們必須修正一下資訊，活動將在晚上8點開始，不是7點。請接受我們犯下錯誤的道歉。我們知道您必須再次安排您的行程。很抱歉為您帶來不便。

誠摯地，

李

Chapter
1

Part 1
Part 2
Part 3
Part 4
Part 5

社交邀請 Social invitations

Part 6
Part 7

重點單字 記起來，寫信回信超精準

① **to feel at home** ph. 感到放鬆
I never feel at home when I am at work.
→上班的時候我總是無法感到放鬆。

② **fantastic** adj. 極棒的、絕佳的
This is such a fantastic movie that I want to watch it again. →這部電影太棒了，我想再看一次。

③ **correction** n. 更正、修正
I still have several grammar corrections to make in this paper. →這篇論文中我還有幾個文法需要做修正。

④ **rearrange** v. 重新排列、重新整理
Can you help me rearrange the documents together?
→你可以幫我一起整理這些文件嗎？

Unit 09 | 婉拒邀請信函

要拒絕**對方的邀請**時，該怎麼寫呢？

Dear Rose,

Thank you for your invitation for the 10th anniversary event of your company.

However, I am very sorry to tell you that on that day, I should be in Texas, America for an important **seminar**. I am afraid that it is **impossible** for me to make it to your event. I wish you a successful celebration.

Yours faithfully,

Denny Li

親愛的羅斯：

謝謝你邀請我參加你們公司成立十週年的慶典。

然而，很遺憾的告訴你，我那天將在美國德州參加一場很重要的研討會。我恐怕不能參加你們的活動了。預祝你們的慶典成功。

誠摯地，

丹尼‧李

Chapter

1

Part 1
Part 2
Part 3
Part 4
Part 5

社交邀請 Social invitations

Part 6
Part 7

收到對方**婉拒邀請**的信時，該怎麼回呢？ — □ ✕

Dear Denny,

It's a pity that you can't come. Hope we won't miss you next time.

Yours,

Rose

親愛的丹尼：

很遺憾你不能來。希望下次還有機會邀情您。

誠摯地，

羅斯

不同的答覆還可以怎麼回呢？ — □ ✕

Dear Denny,

The reason I wrote to you again is that our anniversary is **postponed** to the next weekend. We wonder if you can come then. We'll send out **revised** invitation. Hope to see you at our celebration event!

Sincerely,

Rose

親愛的丹尼：

我再次寫信給您，是因為我們的慶典延後到下週末。不知到時您是否有時間。我們會再次寄出修改日期後的邀請函。希望能在慶祝活動上見到您！

誠摯地，

羅斯

重點單字記起來,寫信回信超精準

① **seminar** n. 討論會、研討會
This is a seminar on transitional justice.
→這是一場關於轉型正義的研討會。

② **impossible** adj. 不可能的、做不到的
It's impossible for the little boy to climb up that tall tree. →小男孩不可能爬上那棵高樹。

③ **postpone** v. 使延期、延緩
She postpones the meeting for personal reasons.
→她因私人因素將會議延期。

④ **revise** v. 修改、修正
The script was revised several times before made into a movie. →在拍成電影前,劇本歷經多次修改。

Unit 10 | 取消邀請信函

要**取消邀請**時，該怎麼寫呢？ ─ □ ✕

Dear Mr. Affleck,

I am terribly sorry to tell you that our project of B software development has been cancelled. I just heard that RDC company has made a successful development and prepared to **launch** it into the market by next month. Our client has already **terminated** the contract with us.

Therefore, we have to **suspend** our cooperation on the project and **cancel** our invitation for collaboration. As soon as I found a new project, I will contact you immediately.

Please forgive our last-minute change and notice.

Sincerely yours,

Will Smith

親愛的艾佛列克先生：

非常抱歉的通知您我們開發B軟體的專案已經被取消了。我剛剛獲知RDC公司已經成功的開發了該軟體，並準備好在下個月進入市場。我們的客戶已經和我們中止了協議。

因此，我們不得不將我們的專案合作事宜暫緩，並取消我們的合作邀約。一旦我找到新的項目，我會立即和您聯繫。

請原諒我們在最後一刻的變動及倉促的通知。

誠摯地，

威爾・史密斯

Dear Will,

What a pity that we cannot work together! But I believe we can cooperate in the near future.

Yours truly,

Affleck

親愛的威爾：

不能一起工作真是遺憾！但我相信在不久的將來我們一定會再次合作。

誠摯地，

艾佛列克

Dear Will,

It's ok. In fact, there's another project offer for me at hand and it requires an expert team. So, would you like receive a collaboration invitation from me this time?

Yours truly,

Affleck

親愛的威爾：

沒關係。事實上，有另一個項目來找我。這個項目需要組成一個專業團隊。這次願意換你接受我的合作邀請嗎？

誠摯地，

艾佛列克

Chapter

1

Part 1

Part 2

Part 3

Part 4

Part 5

社交邀請 Social invitations

Part 6

Part 7

重點單字 記起來，寫信回信超精準

① **launch** ⓥ 開始、展開、投放市場

The protestors are going to launch another demonstration.

→抗議人士將發起另一場遊行。

② **terminate** ⓥ 終止、結束

Due to unpleasant negotiations, they terminated the contract. →因不愉快的協商，他們終止了合約。

③ **suspend** ⓥ 懸掛、使暫停

My little brother was suspended from school for misbehavior.

→我弟弟因行為不當被休學了。

④ **cancel** ⓥ 取消、刪除

After the big fight, the two canceled the wedding.

→因為大吵，他倆取消了婚禮。

Unit 01 | 公司隆重開幕

想祝賀**對方開業**時，該怎麼寫呢？　　　

Dear Mr. Brown,

We have just learned that your Office in Hong Kong will be opened and ready for business. Please accept our deepest congratulations. We,MLSCo., wish you every success in this highly **competitive** international market.

With your **expertise** and proven capability in finance, I can be sure that your **venture** will be a huge success.

We are looking forward to our future cooperation.

Should there be any way in which we can be of assistance, please do not hesitate to contact me personally.

Sincerely yours,
Alice White
CEO

親愛的布朗先生：

我們剛剛得知櫃公司的香港分布即將開張營業，恭賀貴公司香港分部的盛大開業，我們MLS公司預祝貴公司在競爭激烈的國際市場上，能有非凡的成就。

在您的英明領導下，貴公司定能大展宏圖。期待未來能與您合作。

如能有所幫助，請儘管與我私下聯繫。

真誠地，
CEO
愛麗絲‧懷特

Chapter
1

Part 1
Part 2
Part 3
Part 4
Part 5
Part 6
Part 7

恭喜祝賀 Congratulations

收到祝賀開業的信時，該**怎麼回**呢？　　— □ ✕

Dear Mr. White,

As the CEO of DHC Finance, I am writing to thank you personally for your company's congratulations and support in Hong Kong office-establishing effort.Thank you very much!

Please convey my sincere thanks to all of those other people in your company who contributed in any way to the DHC Co.

I am looking forward to seeing you at the EconomyForum next month in Taipei and have an **in-depth** discussion on our future cooperation.

Yours sincerely,

Carol Brown

親愛的懷特先生：

我謹代表 DHC 公司向貴公司的道賀表示感謝，並感謝貴公司在我香港分部籌備階段給予的大力幫助。

請向貴公司曾經協助過 DHC 公司的其他員工轉達我們的謝意。

經濟論壇將於下月在台北舉行，我期待屆時與您的會面深入探討兩方下一步的合作。

誠摯地，

凱羅・布朗

不同的答覆還可以怎麼回呢？　　— □ ✕

Mr. White,

Please allow me to extend my personal thanks on behalf of the DHC Company to your congratulationon our new Hong Kong Office.

Sincerely thank you for supporting us for ever since our first collaboration and wish there is still a door open for our future corporation.

Sincerely yours,

Carol Brown

親愛的布朗先生：

請允許我代表 DHC 公司向貴公司表示感謝。感謝貴公司對我香港分部成立的道賀。

衷心的感謝您自我們第一次合作以來的支持，並希望未來仍有合作發展的空間。

誠摯地，

凱羅・布朗

 重點單字記起來，寫信回信超精準

① **competitive** adj. 競爭性的
Both Chinese New Year and Christmas are highly competitive sales seasons.
→農曆新年和耶誕節將都是激烈競爭的銷售季。

② **expertise** n. 專業技能、專門知識
His expertise in mathematics has contributed greatly to the society. →他在數學方面的專長大大貢獻社會。

③ **venture** n. 冒險、投機
The medical staff ventured their lives to save the patients. →醫療團隊冒生命危險拯救病人。

④ **in-depth** adj. 深度的、深入的
The in-depth discussions on literature has surely enriched my spirit. →深度的文學探討真的充實了我的心靈。

Unit 02 | 祝賀職位晉升

恭喜**對方升遷**時，該怎麼寫呢？

Dear Smith,

Congratulations on your recent **promotion** to head the Marketing Department of DB Bank.

I know how hard you have worked to earn the recognition from your company. You deserve the position more than anyone else because of your extensive experience, **diligence**, and **resourcefulness**.

Again, congratulations to you, Mr. Smith, and good luck to your new position as the Director of Marketing Department.

Yours sincerely,

Sonia Chen

親愛的史密斯：

祝賀你晉升為DB銀行的行銷部主任。

我深知你為獲得同事的認可是多麼的工作努力。你經驗豐富，勤奮刻苦，知識淵博，你比任何人都更能勝任這份工作。

再一次向你表示祝賀。祝願你在市場部主管這個新職位上工作順利。

誠摯地，

索妮亞陳

189

Dear Sonia,

Thank you for your kind letter congratulating on my promotion.

My new position is actually very demanding; it requires full **commitment**. However, I am determined to do my utmost to tide us over during this difficult time and make the company stronger in every way possible.

I look forward to your continue support.

Yours sincerely,

Smith

親愛的索妮亞：

感謝你的祝賀以及你的鼓勵。

我的新職位要求其實很苛刻，需要我全心投入工作。然而，我會盡最大的努力幫助公司走出困境並使其全方位得到提升。

期盼你一如既往的支持。

誠摯地，

史密斯

Dear Sonia,

I want to extend my thanks to your congratulation message. I am very delighted to get it from an old friend like you.

You can be sure this is the best gift I've ever received, and I will treat it as a good transition for my new career.

Best regards to you and your family.

Sincerely yours,

Smith

Chapter
1

Part 1
Part 2
Part 3
Part 4
Part 5
Part 6
Part 7

恭喜祝賀 Congratulations

親愛的索妮亞：

謝謝你的祝賀。能得到像你這樣的老朋友的道賀令我高興不已。

這絕對是我收過最棒的禮物。我將把它視為事業的轉捩點。

祝你和你的家人一切順利。

誠摯地，

史密斯

重點單字記起來，寫信回信超精準

① **promotion** n. 升職、晉升、促進
I heard that you got a promotion last month.
Congratulations! →我聽說你上個月獲得升遷。恭喜！

② **diligence** n. 勤勉、勤奮
With diligence and patience, I'm sure you can achieve anything. →擁有勤奮和耐心，我相信你可以完成任何事。

③ **resourcefulness** n. 足智多謀
As a team leader, he used his resourcefulness and gained a series of success.

→身為隊長，他運用了他的足智多謀贏得多場勝利。

④ **commitment** n. 託付、承諾、信奉
You are new here; you don't have to make such a big commitment. →你是新人，無需做出這麼大的承諾。

Unit 03 | 祝賀榮譽退休

祝賀**他人將榮退**時，確認信該怎麼寫呢？

Dear Roger,

I just heard the news that MLS Company will have to get along without their most outstanding HR manager.

We will miss you, naturally. Everyone that has worked with you truly appreciated your expertise and a good sense of humor.

After dedicating for this company for over 30 years, it's nice to see you come to this point in your life. Tracy and Mike join in wishing for you and your wife, Tina, many happy years in your hometown. Good luck in your **retirement**. Please come by and see us here when you get to Taipei.

Sincerely,

Abby

親愛的羅傑：

我剛剛得知MLS最傑出的人事經理就要光榮退休了。

我們大家都會想念您的。與您打過交道的人都很欣賞您的專業能力及絕佳的幽默感。

在為公司嘔心瀝血30年之後，很高興到了你退休的日子。翠西和麥可與我一起祝您與蒂娜在家鄉生活愉快。祝好運，有空來台北的時候，不要忘記回公司看看我們。

誠摯地，

艾比

Chapter

1

Part 1
Part 2
Part 3
Part 4
Part 5
Part 6
Part 7

恭喜祝賀 Congratulations

收到他人**祝賀榮退**時，該怎麼回呢？　　─ □ ✕

Dear Abby,

Thank you all for all the good wishes to my retirement.

I have been working here, MLS Company,for over 30 years and the time has come for me **to bid farewell** to all of you.

MLS Company is such a sweet place where I was taught to deal with difficulties and challenges, from which I witnessed my failures and successes. I have spent some of the best time of my life here, and MLS will continue to hold a special place in my heart and will **accompany** me in the rest of my life.

I am grateful to all of you, my colleagues, for your support during all these years. Thanks again.

Tina and I wish the **prosperity** of the company and send our best regards to you all.

Sincerely,

Roger

......

親愛的艾比：

謝謝大家在我退休臨別時給予我的祝福。

我在MLS工作了30年，現在是說再見的時候了。

MLS是如此溫馨的一個大家庭，我在這裡學會了如何去面對困難，迎接挑戰，見證了我的挫敗和成功。我人生中目前最好的時光都是在MLS度過的。這段記憶將在我的心中佔據特別的位置，並將伴我度過今後的時光。

我非常感激你們在過去的日子裡給予我的一切幫助。再次感謝。

我的妻子蒂娜與我一同祝願公司蒸蒸日上，祝福大家萬事如意。

誠摯地，

羅傑

Dear Abby,

Please accept my heartiest thanks for your good wishes to my retirement.

It is really difficult to believe that I am going to retire after serving 30 years in MLS Company, which has built me my entire career. I have spent many pleasant moments with you as well as other colleagues, and I would like to thank you through this opportunity for the incredible support that you have provided me for the past few years. It was you, along with all of my colleagues, who made my days in MLS meaningful.

My best wishes for the prosperity of MLS Company and to you all.

Sincerely yours,

Roger

親愛的艾比：

請接受我最誠懇的謝意，感謝對我退休的祝福。

我在MLS工作了30年後即將退休，這真令人難以置信。我與你們大家一起度過了一段美好的時光。我會永遠珍視這份對我意義非凡的回憶。

我想藉此機會對你們在過去的日子裡給予我的大力支持表示感謝。正是你們，讓我在MLS的日子變得有意義。

祝公司前程似錦，祝大家萬事如意。

誠摯地，

羅傑

Chapter
1

Part 1
Part 2
Part 3
Part 4
Part 5
Part 6
Part 7

恭喜祝賀 Congratulations

 重點單字記起來，寫信回信超精準

① **retirement** n. 退休
After retirement, she spent most of her time playing chess. →退休之後，她花大部分的時間下棋。

② **to bid farewell** ph. 道別、告別
To bid farewell, I gave him a long and warm hug.

→為了道別，我給了他一個長而暖的擁抱。

③ **accompany** v. 陪伴、伴隨
My sister asked me to accompany to go to the bathroom last night. →我妹妹昨晚要我陪她上廁所。

④ **prosperity** n. 興旺、繁榮
The early 20th century was far from a time of peace and prosperity. →二十世紀初期一點都不算是和平及繁榮的時代。

Unit 04 | 營收表現良好

想祝賀對方**賺取利潤**時，該怎麼寫呢？

Dear Mark,

Congratulations! According to a business report, your company is making huge profits now. It's such a thrill to know that. We should definitely get together to celebrate it.

Being your friend for so many years, I always trust your ability and **insight**. When you showed me around your company last year, I noticed that everything is well-organized and the employees are working really hard in the **workspace**. Ever since then, I have told everybody around me that you can make it. Time proves everything. I believe that your company can continue to **advance** under your leadership.

Yours,

Ross

親愛的馬克：

恭喜你！有商業報導指出你的公司現在已經開始盈利了。這太令人振奮了。我們應該找一天一起慶祝慶祝。

作為多年的朋友，我一直相信你的能力和洞察力。去年你帶我參觀貴公司的時候，我就發現，公司裡一切井然有序，員工也很努力。從那以後，我就告訴身邊所有的人，你肯定會成功的。時間已經證明了。我相信，在你的領導下，貴公司將不斷壯大。

真誠地，

羅斯

Chapter

1

Part 1
Part 2
Part 3
Part 4
Part 5
Part 6
Part 7

恭喜祝賀 Congratulations

收到對方**祝賀獲利**表現的信時，該怎麼回呢？ — □ ✕

Dear Ross,

Thank you very much. The report is right. I was also excited when I learned that my company is making profits.

Before reaching this state, I have little knowledge on **start-up** operations. During the past few years, I had to learn everything by myself through endless mistakes. Now, my efforts finally paid off.

Thanks for your support.

Yours, Mark

....

親愛的羅斯：

非常感謝。報導說的沒錯。當我得知公司開始盈利時，我也很激動。

在此之前，我對新創公司的營運幾乎一無所知。過去這些年，為了這個新公司，我需要從無數的錯誤中自學所有東西。現在，我的努力終於有了回報。

謝謝你的支持。

真誠地，馬克

不同的答覆還可以怎麼回呢？ — □ ✕

Dear Ross,

Thanks for your congratulation. It means so much to me.

I have to admit that it is you that have helped me a lot from the very beginning till now. You are the first person that has listened to my idea and decided to invest me. I'm deeply grateful to you.

Yours, Mark

親愛的羅斯：

感謝你的祝賀。對我的意義非凡。

我得承認，是你自始自終都在幫助我。你是第一位聽取我的想法的人，也是第一位決定投資給我的。對此，我深表感激。

真誠地，馬克

 重點單字 記起來，寫信回信超精準

① **insight** n. 洞察力、判斷力
His success can be ascribed to his profound insight.
→他的成功可歸功於他深刻的洞察力。

② **workspace** n. 工作空間
I aim to create a harmonious workspace.
→我旨在創造和諧的工作空間。

③ **advance** v. 前進、促進、進步
The team has advanced in its integration of various industry knowledge. →此團隊在不同產業知識上的整合有了進步。

④ **start-up** n. 新創公司
Taiwan Startup Stadium is famous for its teaching for startup operations.
→台灣新創競技場以其對新創營運的教學聞名。

Unit 05 | 工作表現出色

想讚美對方的**工作表現**時，該怎麼寫呢？

Dear Frank,

On behalf of the Marketing Dept, I would like to extend my congratulation to you. The advertising idea you came up with for the "Christmas Season" promotion is excellent. Good news from our sales team is that they have received **unanimous** favors from our clients.

Undoubtedly, your outstanding performance will improve employee **morale** against the **stagnant** economy. Your recent contribution will be of great importance to our company and the admiration for your accomplishments is felt by all of us.

We are looking forward to your persistent efforts.

Again, congratulations on a well-done job.

Sincerely yours,
Tim Clinton

Marketing Dept Manager

親愛的法蘭克：

我謹代表行銷部向你表示祝賀。你為對即將到來的聖誕季促銷提出的廣告創意十分出色。從銷售部傳來的好消息是你的創意得到了客戶的一致好評。

在如今經濟低迷的大環境下，你的出色表現無疑會提升全體員工的士氣。你為公司做出的貢獻有很大的意義，我們對你心存景仰。

期待你在今後的工作中再接再厲。

再一次祝賀你的出色表現。

誠摯地，
行銷部經理

提姆・克林頓

回覆對方讚美自己的工作表現時，該怎麼回呢？ — □ ✕

Dear Mr. Clinton,

Thank you for your congratulation message.

I would like to express my gratitude to you for offering me this opportunity to show my potential for the benefit of our company.

I owe my success to the assistance of Christina, Bob, and especially you. It was Christina who inspired me and Bob who helped me in collecting related information. You were the one who helped me deal with difficulties with your expertise and suggestions.

May the Christmas Season Promotion a success.

Sincerely yours,

Frank

....

親愛的克林頓先生：

感謝您來信祝賀。

十分感激您的賞識。使我有機會展示自己的實力為公司謀福利。

我這次的成功是與大家的協助分不開的。克莉斯汀啟發了我的我靈感，包柏幫助我搜集了相關資訊。特別是您的建議和意見幫我解決了一些棘手的問題。

祝願我們的聖誕季促銷大獲成功。

誠摯地

法蘭克

Chapter
1

Part 1
Part 2
Part 3
Part 4
Part 5
Part 6
Part 7

恭喜祝賀 Congratulations

不同的答覆 還可以怎麼回呢？ — □ ✕

Dear Mr. Clinton,

With this letter I want to convey my deepest gratitude for your supportive words and your appreciation of my work. I sincerely thank you for providing me with this brilliant opportunity to show my advertising talent on this project.

I owe my present achievement to all of you. Thank you for your incredible help, patience, and trust. Thank you again.

Sincerely yours,
Frank

親愛的克林頓先生：

感謝你的鼓勵以及對於我工作的肯定。衷心的感謝您讓我在此次項目中發揮我的廣告創意。

創意大獲成功，功勞應當歸功於你們大家。感謝大家給予的大力支持，耐心以及信心。再次感謝。

誠摯地，
法蘭克

 重點單字 記起來，寫信回信超精準

① **unanimous** adj. 全體一致的; 一致同意的; 無異議的
So far, we are unanimous in the adjustment of company policies. →目前為止，我們一直同意公司策略的調整。

② **morale** n. 士氣、鬥志
The bonus surely boosted the department's morale.
→獎金確實振奮了部門的士氣。

③ **stagnant** adj. 蕭條的、不景氣的
During the period of disease control, business is usually stagnant. →在防疫期間，生意通常都不好。

Unit 06 | 祝賀同事生日

要祝賀**同事生日**時，該怎麼寫呢？

Dear Tony,

I hope your birthday is a happy one. We appreciate your work here at MLS Company and hope that we enjoy many more birthdays together.

Since I can not come to your party tomorrow, I send my best wishes in advance. May you have a prosperous future!

I hope my letter and present can show you my heartfelt congratulations on your birthday.

Happy birthday to you!

Sincerely,

Abby

親愛的托尼：

祝你生日快樂！我很高興與你在ABC公司共事，希望能與你一同慶祝你今後的生日。

鑒於明天不能前去你的生日派對道賀，在這裡提前送上我的祝福。願你的未來富足！

我真誠希望我的賀信和禮物能表達我誠心的祝福。

祝你生日快樂！

誠摯地，

艾比

Chapter

1

Part 1
Part 2
Part 3
Part 4
Part 5
Part 6
Part 7

恭喜祝賀 Congratulations

回覆同事的**生日祝賀**信時，該怎麼寫呢？ — □ ✕

Dear Abby,

It is so **considerate** of you to remember my birthday and send me your carefully-selected birthday present. You could not have given me anything that I wanted more.

It's a pity that we couldn't enjoy the celebration together. I sincerely hope that we could get together some time after the business trip so that I can thank you personally.

Thank you again.

Best wishes,

Tony

親愛的艾比：

你如此貼心的記得我的生日。謝謝你送給我一份精心挑選的禮物，那是我最想收到的。很遺憾我們沒能一起慶祝。我真誠的希望在你出公差之後我們一起聚一聚。再次感謝！

誠摯地，

托尼

不同的答覆還可以怎麼回呢？ — □ ✕

Dear Abby,

Thank you for your congratulation card and your birthday gift. You can not imagine how excited I was when I opened the **package** this morning and saw the **handsome** baseball cap. It was so sweet of you to give me such a wonderful gift. It's a **pity** that you can not come tomorrow and see how well I look in it. I do hope to see you soon.

Thanks a lot!

Regards,

Tony

親愛的艾比：

謝謝你的生日賀卡以及生日禮物。你無法想像我早上拆開包裝看到這頂帥氣的棒球帽時那興奮的樣子。你能送我這麼棒的一件禮物太貼心了。但可惜的是你明天不能前來看到戴著帽子的我多帥。希望能快點見到你。

萬分感謝！

誠摯地，

托尼

重點單字記起來，寫信回信超精準

① **considerate** adj. 體貼的、體諒的、考慮周到的
What a considerate holiday plan!
→多麼體貼的旅遊計畫！

② **package** n. 包裹、一包
I opened the package happily only to find a broken vase. →我開心地打開包裹，結果發現花瓶破掉了。

③ **handsome** adj. 漂亮的、帥氣的、美觀的
My parents gave me a handsome graduation present.
→我爸媽給我一份很好的畢業禮物。

④ **pity** n. 同情、可惜
It's a pity that our trip to Hong Kong was canceled.
→可惜我們的香港行被取消了。

Unit 07 | 賀年度員工獎

要恭賀**同事獲獎**時，該怎麼寫呢？　　　— □ ✕

Dear Vera,

Congratulations on winning the prize of the Best Employee for theYear. Your excellent performance was **validated** by all the staff in our company. Although you and your team always work quietly, everyone in the office can observe your efficient and heartfelt service and no one can imagine how without our administration team we can keep this office operation smoothly.

I hope our **bonus** can motivate you and your team to deliver good service continuously.

Sincerely yours,

Leonard Dylan

親愛的薇拉：

祝賀你獲得公司今年的年度最佳員工獎。我們公司所有員工都見證了你的優秀表現。雖然你和你的團隊總是默默的工作著，這個辦公室裡的每個人依然能夠觀察到你們有效率而貼心的服務。沒有人能夠想像出要是沒有我們公司的行政團隊，這個辦公室該如何正常平穩地運轉。

我希望獎金能夠鼓勵你的你的團隊繼續提供無限的優質服務。

真誠地，

李奧納多・迪倫

收到獲獎祝賀信時，該**怎麼回**呢？　　　— □ ✕

Dear Mr. Dylan,

I feel grateful to receive this honor from you. It makes me feel needed and inspires me to work harder.

I will continue to dedicate myself to this company.

Sincerely yours,

Vera

親愛的迪倫先生：

您給我這個獎我非常感激，它讓我覺得被需要，鼓勵我更努力的工作。

我會繼續將全部的熱情投入到工作中。

真誠地，

薇拉

不同的答覆還可以怎麼回呢？　　　— □ ✕

Dear Mr. Dylan,

Thanks for **granting** me such **recognition**. I feel proud to work in this company.

The honor is not just for me but for my whole team. I can do nothing without anyone of them. I will share with them this great honor.

Sincerely yours,

Vera

親愛的迪倫先生：

謝謝您授予我這個獎，我自豪能服務於這間公司。

Chapter
1

Part 1
Part 2
Part 3
Part 4
Part 5
Part 6
恭喜祝賀 Congratulations
Part 7

這份榮譽不是我一個人的，它屬於我們整個團隊，一旦缺少他們其中任何一個，我寸步難行。因此我會和他們分享這份喜悅。

真誠地，

薇拉

重點單字記起來，寫信回信超精準

① **validate** ⓥ 證實、使有效
You can ask the receptionist to validate your parking.
→你可以請櫃檯人員幫你驗證停車。

② **bonus** ⓝ 獎金、紅利、額外津貼
As soon as he received a bonus, he booked a ticket to Japan. →當他領到獎金之後，他就訂了去日本的機票。

③ **grant** ⓥ 授予、承認、允許
I was finally granted the pension I was promised.
→我終於領到我被承諾會拿到的退休金了。

④ **recognition** ⓝ 認出、承認、認可
I earn the recognition of the professor by hard work.
→我用努力認真贏得了教授的認可。

Unit 01 | 新員工到職日

宣佈新員工今日到職時，該怎麼寫呢？ — □ X

Dear all,

I am very delighted to make the **announcement** about our new colleague, Jasmine Lee, who has just joined our team today.

Jasmine graduated from Tainan University this summer and she will **replace** Kate Becksonas as our department secretary. Please join me to welcome Jasmine as our new team member and **pursue** a new development with us.

Sincerely yours,

Robbin Williams

Marketing Director

大家好，

我很高興地向大家宣佈一個好休息，今天有一位新同事，賈斯敏‧李加入我們部門。

賈斯敏今年夏天剛剛從台南大學畢業。她將接替凱特‧貝克森擔任本部門秘書。請和我一起歡迎賈斯敏的加入，與我們並肩發展。

真誠地，

羅賓‧威廉姆斯

行銷部總監

Chapter
1

Part 1
Part 2
Part 3
Part 4
Part 5
Part 6
Part 7

職位變更 Personnel change

收到**新職員**到職的信，該怎麼回呢？   — □ ✕

Dear Mr. Williams,

We are really glad that Jasmine is **on board** now, and to show our warm welcome to Jasmine, we decide to have dinner together today after work. Please kindly join us.

Yours sincerely,

Jack Ross

··

親愛的威廉姆斯先生：

我們很高興賈斯敏今天任職。為了表示我們的熱烈歡迎，我們決定今晚下班後去聚餐。誠摯的邀請您加入我們。

真誠地，

傑克・羅斯

不同的答覆還可以怎麼回呢？   — □ ✕

Dear Jasmine,

Welcome on board!

Since we're expecting you for 2 weeks, we decide to have dinner together today, after work of course.Don't be nervous. We want to get to know you better and introduce you more about this company.

Looking forward to your reply!

Yours,

Jack Ross

··

親愛的賈斯敏：

歡迎！

我們期待你兩週後你終於來了，因此我們決定今晚下班後聚餐。別緊張，我們想多瞭解你，並向你多介紹這間公司。

期待你的回覆！

誠摯地，

傑克‧羅斯

 重點單字記起來，寫信回信超精準

① **announcement** n. 通告、宣告、公告、發表
Everyone was astonished at the new announcement in the annual meeting.
→每個人都對年度會議上的新宣告感到震驚。

② **replace** v. 取代、替換
No one can replace you in my heart.
→沒有人能取代你在我心裡的位置。

③ **pursue** v. 追求、追趕、從事
Pursuing a career of literature studies is my lifelong dream. →追求文學研究的事業是我畢生的夢想。

④ **on board** ph. 上船、開始工作
Welcome on board!
→歡迎加入！

Unit 02 | 向上提出辭呈

要提出**離職申請**時，該怎麼寫呢？

Dear Mr. Smith,

I am regret to **tender** my **resignation** to you. This is definitely a hard decision for me. I've had a wonderful experience in my career life in ICG company. However, I have decided to take a new challenge in another company. I would also like to express my gratitude for your support and guidance in last three years.

Wish you all the best and wish our company a bright future.

Truly yours,

Ivan Marcel

親愛的史密斯先生：

我非常遺憾地向您提交我的辭呈。這對我來說絕對是個艱難的決定。我在ICG公司的經歷是我工作生涯中精彩的一筆。然而，我已經決定到另外一家公司接受一個新的挑戰。我還想感謝您在過去三年中對我的支持與指導。

祝您萬事如意，祝願本公司前途光明。

真誠地，

伊旺・馬歇爾

Dear Ivan,

I feel sorry to lose a brilliant staff like you. You did very well in the past 3 years.However, I know you are a determined person.It's hard to persuade you to continue working with us. I also thank you for your dedication. Wish you all the best.

Yours ever,

Smith

親愛的伊旺：

要失去你這麼聰明的員工我真捨不得。過去的三年裡你一直很出色。但我知道你是個很堅定的人，很難說服你留下來繼續與我們共事。我也要謝謝你的貢獻。祝福你。

真誠地，

史密斯

Dear Ivan,

I wonder the reason why you want to **depart** from us. **Dissatisfied** with the salary? Want a promotion? Or too much restrictions?

No matter what reason is, I want to know your honest answer. If it's the reason listed above, I can do something for you.

Yours ever,

Smith

Chapter
1

Part 1
Part 2
Part 3
Part 4
Part 5
Part 6
Part 7

職位變更 Personnel change

親愛的伊旺：

我想知道你想離開的原因。不滿現在的薪水？想要升職？或是太多限制？

不管是什麼原因，我都想聽到你誠實的回答。如果是以上所列的原因，我會為你解決的。

真誠地，

史密斯

重點單字記起來，寫信回信超精準

① **tender** 提出、提供、投標
After several major setbacks, I decided to tender my resignation. →在數個重大挫敗之後，我決定提出我的辭呈。

② **resignation** 辭職書、辭呈、順從、屈從
They accepted her resignation reluctantly.
→他們無奈地接受了她的辭呈。

③ **depart** 離開、出發、起程、違反、去世
He never come back since departed from home 30 years ago. →他自從30年前離開家就再也沒有回來過。

④ **dissatisfied** 不滿意的
I'm very dissatisfied with your recent work performance. →我對你最近的工作表現非常不滿意。

Unit 03 | 回復崗位通知

Dear Michael,

I hope everything goes well with you. I just want to share with you a piece of good news that I am **recovered** from the **stomach flu**, and I plan to go back to work on the coming Monday. I also heard that your promotion of HR manager has been announced.Congratulations! I cannot wait to re-join our team and work with you again.

Many thanks for your **comforting** wordsduring my sick leave. I am looking forward to returning to our office.

Sincerely yours,

Jenny Lopez

親愛的邁克爾:

希望你一切順利,我只是想告訴你一個好消息,我的腸胃炎已經好了。我計畫下週一開始回去上班。我聽説你晉升為人力資源經理的消息已經宣布了,恭喜!我真等不及要回到我們的團隊中,和你一起工作了。

非常感謝你在我生病期間的慰問,我期望著回到公司。

真誠地,

珍妮・洛佩茲

Chapter

1

Part 1
Part 2
Part 3
Part 4
Part 5
Part 6
Part 7

職位變更 Personnel change

收到員工將**回復崗位**的信時，該怎麼回呢？ — □ ✕

Dear Jenny,

The good news **inspires** everyone.We miss you so much, and we realized how important you are when you are away from us.

Can't wait to see you next Monday.

Yours faithfully,

Michael

親愛的珍妮：

好消息振奮了所有人，我們太想你了。當你不在我們身邊的時候我們才意識到你有多重要。

簡直等不及下週一見到你。

真誠地，

邁克爾

不同的答覆還可以怎麼回呢？ — □ ✕

Dear Jenny,

It's great to hear that you are fully recovered from the sickness, and it's ok if you want to take a few more days to rest. Health is much more important than work.

Yours faithfully,

Michael

親愛的珍妮：

聽到你完全康復了，實在太好了。但如果你想多休息幾天也沒問題。身體可比工作重要多了。

真誠地，

邁克爾

重點單字記起來，寫信回信超精準

① **recover** **v.** 重新找到、恢復
I'm not fully recovered from the flu.
→我的流感還沒完全好。

② **stomach flu** **ph.** 腸胃炎
Amy got a stomach flu and called in sick today.
→艾咪得了腸胃炎，今天請病假。

③ **comforting** **adj.** 安慰的、令人寬慰的
I have to say that her card is comforting to all of us now. →我必須說她的卡片令我們所有人感到安慰。

④ **inspire** **v.** 鼓舞、激發、使產生靈感
The film inspired me to write a script on a long road trip. →這部電影激發我寫一個長途公路旅行的劇本。

Unit 04 | 出國進修申請

想要**詢問面試**的結果時，該怎麼寫呢？

Dear Kevin,

As the leader of Marketing Department, I think it isurgent to express my concerns about the **enhancement** of our **professionalism**.

More and more newcomers are enteringthis industry with **advanced** marketing knowledge and experiences, those competitors' outstanding marketing performance has threatenedour business seriously. I believe better skills will help our team to provide better service to our clients.

In order to achieve this goal, I think it is necessary for our team to learn more about customer **insight** and marketing strategic planning. Therefore, I apply for three opportunities for our selected team members to study abroad.

I guarantee that these three members willl earn hard and come back to contribute for our company's bright future with their solid knowledge on the above-mentioned two aspects. Your decision will influence both our company's and our marketing department's future. Please kindly consider it.

Looking forward to your approval.

Best regards,

Michael

親愛的凱文：

作為行銷部的部門主管，我急迫地想要表達關於我們專業性提高的擔憂。

越來越多行業新進者帶著他們領先的市場行銷知識和經驗進入我們產業，這些競爭對手在市場上的出色表現已經對我們的生意造成很大威脅。我相信我們團隊成員有了更好的技能才能夠為我們的客戶提供更好的服務。

為了實現這個目標，我想有必要派遣團隊成員去學習消費者洞察和行銷策略規劃。因此，我申請3個出國深造的機會給我們挑選出來的團隊成員。

我保證這3位同事會努力學習，並且在回國後為我們公司的美好未來做出更大的貢獻。您的決定可能會影響公司和行銷部門的未來，請您慎重考慮。

期待您的批覆。

祝福您，

麥克爾

收到**出國進修**的申請時，該怎麼回呢？　　　— □ ✕

Dear Michael,

I totally agree with you and I will take this into further consideration. Could you please write a more detailed report or plan? Thanks.

Yours,

Kevin

親愛的麥克爾：

我完全同意你的看法，我進一步考慮這件事。你能寫一份更詳細的報告或計畫嗎？謝謝。

誠摯地，

凱文。

Chapter

1

Part 1
Part 2
Part 3
Part 4
Part 5
Part 6
Part 7

職位變更 Personnel change

不同的答覆 還可以怎麼回呢？ — □ ✕

Dear Michael,

I appreciate your effort towards the future of this young company. However, as you know, at present, we don't have the capacity to start such a program for employees to study abroad.

Yours,

Kevin

親愛的麥克爾：

感謝你對這間創立不久的公司的未來發展做出的努力。但如你所知，目前公司沒有能力開展這項計畫讓員工出國。

誠摯地，

凱文

 重點單字 記起來，寫信回信超精準

① **enhancement** n. 提升、增加
I always strive to seek enhancement of my language ability. →我總是追求提升我的語言能力。

② **professionalism** n. 專業技術、專業度
To show my professionalism, I'll demonstrate the procedure for you. →為展現我的專業，我會展示程序給你們看。

③ **advanced** adj. 先進的、高級的
I'm going to take the advanced level of mathematics test in June. →我將在六月參加高級數學的測驗。

④ **insight** n. 洞察力、洞悉、眼光
Her lecture provided us an insight into the issue of gender equality. →她的演講使我們對於性別平等的議題有了更深一層的理解。

Note

Chapter 2
出國留學萬事通

Unit 01 | 國外留學申請

想寄信給外國學校**申請就讀**時，該怎麼寫呢？ ─ □ ✕

Dear Sir or Madam,

I would like to apply to attend the International Law Master Program in your university this September. I am planning to graduate from National Taiwan University this July and I will receive a bachelor degree in Law.

I have always expected to join Boston University as it is world-famous for its strong leadership in the field of Law. I believe I will have a great time **enriching** my knowledge and professionalism there.

Per your request, I have attached my recommendation letter, a copy of my university **transcript**, a copy of my TOEFL certificate, and my application form for the program.

Thanks in advance for your consideration and I am looking forward to your response soon.

Sincerely yours,

Ling Li

親愛的先生／女士：

我想申請貴校今年9月開學的國際法學碩士課程。我將於今年7月自國立台灣大學畢業，並取得法律學士學位。

我一直以來都期待到波士頓大學求學。貴校在法律領域的領導力享譽全球，我相信我將度過一段美好的時光，充實自身知識和專業。

Chapter
2

Part 1

申請準備 Applications

Part 2
Part 3
Part 4
Part 5
Part 6
Part 7

按照貴校的要求，我隨信寄上我的推薦信、大學成績單副本，一份託福成績單副本，以及我的入學申請表。非常感謝您對我的申請予以考慮。期待能儘快收到您的回覆。

真誠地，
林立

收到**國際學生申請就讀**的信時，該怎麼回呢？ — □ ✕

Dear Lin Li,

Thank you for your interest in our university. I am very pleased to inform you that we have decided to accept your application. Please check our **enrollment** procedureon our website and prepare your materials based on the regulations.

Please feel free to contact our administrationoffice through 001- 617-353-2786 if you have any question.

Yours sincerely,

Helen Anderson

親愛的林立同學：

謝謝你對我們大學的關注，我很高興的通知你我們已經決定接受你的入學申請了。請登陸我們的網站查詢入學程式，並根據流程準備你的入學手續。

如有任何問題，請查詢本校行政辦公室，電話：001- 617-353-2786。

真誠地，

海倫・安德森

不同的答覆還可以怎麼回呢？ — □ ✕

Dear Lin Li,

Thanks for being interested in our university; however, I am very sorry to inform you that our class of International Law has been fully-registered. As our Asian Law program is still open for application, if you are interested, we can transfer your application to Asian Law program. Please let us know your decision by June 10, 2020.

We are looking forward to hearing from you.

Regards,

Helen Anderson

親愛的林立同學：

謝謝你對本校的關注，然而，我非常抱歉的說，本校的國際法學班註冊已滿。目前本校的亞洲法學課程還可申請，如果你有興趣，我們將把你的申請轉發到亞洲法學課程。請於2020年6月10日回覆本校你的決定。

期待你的回覆。

真誠地，

海倫・安德森

重點單字記起來，寫信回信超精準

① **enrich** v. 充實、使豐富
Constant reading and exercising enriches my life.
→頻繁的閱讀和運動充實了我的生活。

② **transcript** n. 成績單
Please show your parents the transcript so they know your performance. →請把你的成績單給你的父母看讓他們知道你的表現。

③ **enrollment** n. 登記、註冊
I finally made a successful enrollment to the International Law Program. →我終於成功註冊國際法課程了。

Unit 02 | 學生宿舍資格

想申請**學生宿舍**時，該怎麼寫呢？　　　　－ □ ✕

Dear Dean of Academic Affairs,

I am writing to you to apply for on-campus housing. My name is Ling Li, a new Taiwanese student from the International Law Program. I am now living an apartment which is far away from our university and it has been the one with the least **favorable** rent in town.

As my **financial** situation doesn't allow me to **afford** such an apartment, I would like to apply for a room in the Student Dormitory.

Thanks in advance for your consideration and I sincerely look forward to your approval.

Sincerely yours,

Ling Li

尊敬的教務長：

我來信是想申請學生宿舍。我的名字叫林立，我是一名來自台灣的國際法學班新生。我現在住在一處距離學校很遠的公寓，房租不菲。

由於我的財力不能夠負擔這樣的公寓，我特向您申請入住學生宿舍。

感謝您的考慮，期待您的批准。

真誠地，

林立

Dear Ling Li,

I am sorry to hear about your situation.

After referring to your application, we have decided to arrange a room in the Student Resident Hall 3 for you. Please contact Rose Jansen from Administration Office.Her number is 57349278.She will help you to settle the details.

If you have any further query, feel free to contact me.

Yours sincerely,

Kate Ross

親愛的林立同學：

獲知你的處境後我深感同情。

對於你的學生宿舍申請，經過我們查閱，我們決定在學生公寓3號樓為你安排一個房間。請聯繫行政處的羅斯‧詹森女士，她的電話是57349278，她會幫助你處理細節。

如需其他幫助，請與我聯繫。

真誠地，

凱特‧羅斯

不同的答覆還可以怎麼回呢？ — □ ✕

Dear Ling Li,

I am sorry to hear about your situation.

After refer to your dormitory application, we have considered arranging one room for you. However, as our Student Resident Hall has been fully **occupied** in this semester, we can only list your name on the waiting list for now. As soon as there is a room available, we will notify you to move in.

Chapter

2

Part 1

申請準備 Applications

Part 2
Part 3
Part 4
Part 5
Part 6
Part 7

I am sorry again for the current situation and I appreciate your understanding. If you have any further query, feel free to contact me.

Yours sincerely,

Kate Ross

親愛的林立同學：

聽到你的處境我深感同情。

對於你學生宿舍申請，經過我們認真考慮，我們決定給你安排一個房間。然而，由於本學期學生公寓樓已滿租，我們將你的名字列入了候補名單中，一旦有空出的房間，我們會第一時間通知你入住。

再次對你目前的處境表示抱歉，並感謝你的理解。如需其他幫助，請與我聯繫，

誠摯地，

凱特・羅斯

 重點單字 記起來，寫信回信超精準

① **favorable** adj. 優惠的、贊同的、稱讚的
We decided to offer you the most favorable price.
→我們決定給你一個最優惠的價格。

② **financial** adj. 財政的、金融的、經濟上的
Financial issues have completely wrecked his health condition. →經濟問題毀掉了他的健康。

③ **afford** v. 買得起、支付得起、承擔
We can't afford a lawyer right now.
→我們現在負擔不起律師費用。

④ **occupied** adj. 被佔用的、沒有空間的、有人使用的
I'm sorry the seat is already occupied.
→很抱歉這個座位有人坐了。

Unit 03 | 寄自我推薦信

想寄出**自我推薦信**時，該怎麼寫呢？

Dear Director of Academic Affairs,

I am a Taiwanese student from the International Law program.My name is Ling Li. I am interested in the opening of teaching assistant in our Asian Law department. I have 2 years of teaching assistant experience at the department of Law in National Taiwan University. With my previous work experiences, knowledge in Asian Law, and passion of academic **career**, I believe I am **qualified** for this job. Please **consider** me for the position.

Sincerely looking forward to hearing from you.

Truly yours,

Ling Li

親愛的教務主任：

我是國際法學班的一名台灣學生，我叫林立。我對亞洲法學系的助教空缺非常感興趣。我曾經在國立台灣大學法學部作過兩年助教。憑藉我過往的工作經驗，對於亞洲法的知識，以及對學術事業的熱情，我相信我是這份工作的合適人選。請考慮我的申請。

真誠地期待您的回覆。

林立

Chapter 2

Part 1

申請準備 Applications

Part 2
Part 3
Part 4
Part 5
Part 6
Part 7

收到**自我推薦信**時，該怎麼回呢？　　　— □ ×

Dear Ling Li,

Thank you for your application. After serious consideration and review of your **resume**, we have decided to offer you the job as a teaching assistant in the department of Asian Law. Professor Alex Walter will be your leader.

Please go to Professor Alex Walter's office on 9:00 next Monday morning. He will arrange your work for this position.

If you have any questions, feel free to contact Professor Alex Walter by 38456839. Hope you will work well with Professor Walter.

Yours sincerely,

Kate Ross

親愛的林立：

謝謝你申請亞洲法學部助教的工作。經過認真審閱你的履歷及我們慎重的考慮，我們決定錄用你了，並安排艾里克斯‧懷特爾教授為你的主管。

請於下週一早上9點到他的辦公室報到，他將告訴你在這個職位上的工作內容。

如有任何問題，請聯繫艾里克斯‧懷特爾教授，他的電話是：38456839。希望你和懷特爾教授工作愉快！

真誠地，

凱特‧羅斯

不同的答覆還可以怎麼回呢？　　　　— □ ×

Dear Ling Li,

Thanks for your application for the opening of teaching assistant in Asian Law department. I regret to notify you that we have already found someone more suitable for this position.

I hope there will be other opportunities for you soon.

Yours sincerely,

Kate Ross

親愛的林立同學：

非常感謝你申請亞洲法學部的助教職位。然而，我不得不遺憾地告訴你我們已經找到了一個更適合的人選。

我希望很快會有其他適合你的機會。

真誠地，

凱特・羅斯

重點單字記起來，寫信回信超精準

① **career** n. 職業、事業
She didn't care about her acting career whatsoever.
→她一點都不在乎她的演藝事業。

② **qualified** adj. 合格的、具有資格的
I'm not sure if he is a qualified engineer.
→我不確定他是否是名合格的工程師。

③ **consider** v. 認為、考慮、細想、考慮到
We're considering hiring two more accountants.
→我們在考慮多雇用兩名會計人員。

④ **resume** n. 履歷表
I spent time revising my resume for a promising job interview. →我花時間為了一份具有前景的工作面試修改履歷表。

Unit 04 | 他人推薦信函

要替他人**寫推薦信**時，該怎麼寫呢？

Dear Professor Smith,

I am very pleased to recommend Ling Li to be your teaching assistant. I have known him for five years as his professor in National Taiwan University. He is a brilliant student with outstanding **academic** performances and he was a good team member during the work with our project team. He also **possesses** excellent working attitude. I believe he would be a great talent in any organizations.

Please feel free to contact me if you need any further information. My contact number is 86-21-73963832.

Yours truly,

Liang Ren Chao

史密斯教授：

我非常高興地為您推薦林立同學為您的助教。我和他在國立台灣大學認識，至今有5年時間了。他是一名成績優異的學生，同時，與我們專案小組工作的時侯，他是一個很好的團隊成員。他也擁有非常良好的工作態度。我相信他會成為任何一個機構中的優秀人才。

如果您有任何其他問題，請與我聯繫。我的電話號碼是：86-21-73963832。

真誠地，

趙良人

收到**他人推薦信**時，該怎麼回呢？　　— □ ✕

Dear Chao,

Thank you very much for your recommendation. We will seriously consider his application. Your letter is very helpful to our decision-making of Ling Li's application.

Thanks again for your recommendation.

Regards,

John Smith

親愛的趙：

非常感謝您對林立的推薦。我們會慎重考慮林立的申請。這對於我們針對林立同學的申請審核非常有幫助。

再次感謝您的推薦。

真誠地，

約翰·史密斯

不同的答覆還可以怎麼回呢？　　— □ ✕

Dear Chao,

Thanks for your recommendation of Ling Li. However, in order to have a better and more serious consideration of his application, we need more **concrete** information about his past work experiences in your university. We wonder if you could provide relevant documents about his **responsibilities** back then.

Thank you in advance for your help and looking forward to hearing from you.

Yours sincerely,

John Smith

Chapter
2

Part 1

申請準備 Applications

Part 2
Part 3
Part 4
Part 5
Part 6
Part 7

親愛的趙：

謝謝您對林立在貴校工作經歷和工作表現的證明。然而，為了對他的職位申請做更進一步和謹慎的考量，我們需要一些更具體的資訊。不知您能否告訴我們他當時的具體工作職責？

非常感謝您的協助，期待您的答覆。

真誠地，

約翰・史密斯

 重點單字記起來，寫信回信超精準

① **academic** adj. 學術的、學院的
After finishing my master degree, I know I am not fit for the academic field.
→在結束我的碩士學程之後，我知道我不適合學術領域。

② **possess** v. 擁有、具備
She definitely possesses the skills to conduct this experiment. →她絕對具有執行此實驗的技巧。

③ **concrete** adj. 具體的、實在的
Desks and chairs are concrete objects, while air and light are not. →桌子和椅子是實體物，空氣和光則不是。

④ **responsibility** n. 責任、職責
I undertake the responsibility to supervise the new production line. →我承擔監督新生產線的職責。

Unit 05 | 確認入學通知

要寄出入學通知時，該怎麼寫呢？

Dear Ling Li,

I am very glad to inform you that we have accepted your application for the International Law Program in our university. There are detailed **regulations** regarding new student enrollment on our website. Please prepare needed documents in advance.

If you have any question, please feel free to contact me through the following numbers:

001- 617-353-2786

Yours sincerely,

Helen Anderson

親愛的林立同學：

我很高興地通知您本校國際法計畫已經接受您的入學申請。關於新生入學的規範，請至我們的官方網站查詢，並請提前準備好所需文件。

如您還有其他問題，請隨時撥打下面號碼與我聯繫：

001- 617-353-2786

誠摯地，

海倫・安德森

Chapter

2

Part 1

申請準備 Applications

Part 2
Part 3
Part 4
Part 5
Part 6
Part 7

回覆**入學通知**時，該怎麼寫呢？ — □ ✕

Dear Helen,

Much **gratitude** for your notice. I am very happy to join Boston University and start my **master** degree in the International Law Program. I will do my enrollment preparations accordingly.

Thanks again for your notice, looking forward to seeing you at university.

Yours sincerely,

Ling Li

親愛的海倫：

謝謝你的通知，我對於能夠到波士頓大學入讀國際法碩士課程感到非常高興。我會按照指示做好註冊準備。

再次感謝您的通知，期待與您在學校見面。

真誠地，

林立

不同的答覆還可以怎麼回呢？ — □ ✕

Dear Helen,

Thanks for your notice, I am very happy to join Boston University and start my master degree in International Law. I will prepare needed enrollment materials according to the **instructions** on the website.

Looking forward to seeing from you.

Yours sincerely,

Ling Li

親愛的海倫：

謝謝您發來的入學通知書，我對於能夠到波士頓大學入讀國際法碩士課程感到非常高興。我將根據大學網站的指示說明，做好入學準備工作。

期待見到您。

真誠地，

林立

 重點單字記起來，寫信回信超精準

① **regulation** n. 規則、規範
He didn't conform to the new regulations and was put to jail. →他沒有遵守新規範，因而坐牢。

② **gratitude** n. 感激、感謝
Can't you see that he sent the gift out of gratitude?
→你看不出來他送禮是出自感激之情？

③ **master** n. 碩士（學位）
I finally completed my master's thesis after three years of hard work.
→我終於在三年的辛勤努力之下完成碩士論文。

④ **instruction** n. 指示、命令
The instructions on the manual were unclear and we were all confused.
→手冊上的用法說明模糊不清，我們都很困惑。

Unit 06 | 留學準備工作

要寄出留學準備提醒時，該怎麼寫呢？

Dear Ling Li,

I am very happy to congratulate you that you have been accepted by Boston University. Before you arrive here, I would like to give you to some tips **as follows**:

(1) Carry with you your passport, enrollment letter, receipt, and flight ticket.

(2) Bring USD400 on hand in small **changes** for making phonecalls, taking taxi, and other expenses during the trip.

Wish you a safe trip to Boston.

Yours,
Jane Myer

親愛的林立：

我非常高興的祝賀你被波士頓大學錄取。在你到達之前，我想給你一些小提點。

（1）保管好你的護照、學校的錄取通知書、收據、和機票。

（2）隨身準備400美元現金的零錢，以便你在旅途中打電話、搭計程車和其他的開銷。

祝你在前往波士頓的旅途一路平安！

真誠地，
簡‧梅爾

Dear Jane,

Thank you for your reminder and I will do so **accordingly**. If there is anything else that you think I need to know, please be free to let me know.

Many thanks again for your help.

Yours sincerely,

Ling Li

親愛的簡：

謝謝你的提醒，我會據此做好我的出國準備工作。如果還有什麼其他事您認為我需要瞭解的，請讓我知道。

再次感謝你的幫助。

真誠地，

林立

Dear Jane,

Thanks for your reminder.I would like to, however, ask about the checking-in of the Student Resident Hall. I wonder if you could give me some suggestions regarding what I should prepare **beforehand**.

Many thanks for your help, looking forward to hearing from you.

Yours sincerely,

Ling Li

Chapter
2

Part 1

申請準備 Applications

Part 2
Part 3
Part 4
Part 5
Part 6
Part 7

親愛的簡：

謝謝你的提醒，我會據此做好出國準備工作。不過，入住學生公寓，我想知道針對事前需要準備的東西你是否有什麼建議給我呢？

謝謝你的幫助，期待著你的回覆。

真誠地，

林立

 重點單字記起來，寫信回信超精準

① **as follows** ph. 如下所示
The outcome was as follows: two villages were destroyed and 100 people died.
→結果如下：兩座村莊殞落、一百位民眾喪生。

② **change** n. 零錢
Keep the change. →不用找零。

③ **accordingly** adv. 相應地
Please memorize the dorm rules and behave accordingly.
→請記住宿舍規則並照著做。

④ **beforehand** adv. 事先地、預先地
Don't we need to book the hotel beforehand?
→我們不需要先預訂飯店嗎？

Unit 01 | 搭乘航班誤點

想抱怨**航班誤點**時，該怎麼寫呢？　　　　 — □ ✕

Dear Customer Service Center,

As a customer of your airline, I am very **disappointed** about my recent experience with your company. I booked your flight N399 from Taipei to Boston on last Wednesday. According to the schedule, it supposed to arrive Boston on 18:00.

When I arrived at the airport, I saw that the flight was listed as delayed. I asked the agent immediately for further information. However, the agent responded rudely: "I don't know."

As it is my first time to visit Boston for study, our university **assigned** someone picked me up from the airport because I know no one there. Hence, I am anxious to know the departure and arrival time and connect with the university to re-schedule their pick-up service as well.

After hours of waiting in the airport, my anxiety drove me to check again, I was told then that the flight had been cancelled two hours ago. I believe your company should take full responsibility for the inconvenience and miscommunication I suffered due to the delay.I expect a compensation for it and I await your response within one week.

Sincerely,
Li Ling

親愛的客服中心：

作為你們航空公司的一名乘客，對最近和你們公司之間的經驗非常

Chapter
2

Part 1
Part 2
意外插曲 Accidents

Part 3
Part 4

失望。我預定了上週三從台北到波士頓的N399航班,按計劃應該是 18:00抵達波士頓。

當我抵達機場的時候,看到航班在延誤的名單上。我馬上問代理公司 是不是有進一步的消息,然而代理只粗魯的回覆「不知道」。

因為這是我第一次到波士頓留學。在那我不認識任何人。我的大學承 諾將派車到機場接我。所以我很關心航班起飛和降落的時間。並聯繫 學校重新安排他們的接機服務。

在機場經過數小時的等候,我的焦慮促使我再次詢問代理,但我卻被 告知,航班在2個小時之前就被取消了。我認為你們公司應該就此次 延誤對我造成的不便和不當溝通負全責。我期待你們的賠償,並在一 週之內的回覆。

誠摯地,

林立

收到**航班誤點抱怨**信時,該怎麼回呢? ⎽ ☐ ✕

Dear Ling Li,

Thank you for taking the time to communicate to us about our service problem. We will provide the best solution to resolve your issue as soon as possible.We will contact with you in 3 days to make our best attempt in regaining your confidence in our company.

Please accept our sincerest apology. It is definitely our goal to retain you as a satisfied customer and sincerely hope to serve you again in the future.

Yours truly,

Mary Smith

親愛的林立:

感謝你花費時間和我們溝通服務上的問題。我們將就你的問題儘快提 供滿意的解決方案。我們將在三天後聯繫您並盡我們最大的努力重新 獲得您對我們公司的信心。

請接受我們最誠摯的道歉。我們的目標是能再次贏得您對我們服務的 滿意,也真誠地希望將來可以繼續為您服務。

真誠地,

瑪麗・史密斯

不同的答覆還可以怎麼回呢？ _ □ ✕

Dear Ling Li,

Thank you for the letter, and please accept our sincerest apologies. We plan to compensate with you for the trouble we caused as below:

(a) To upgrade your flight class from economic to business without any additional payment for the following one year.

(b) To double your credits in travel card.

We would like to retain you as a satisfied customer and we do hope to serve you again in future. Hence, please feel free to contact us if you have any further query.

Yours truly,
Mary Smith

親愛的林立：

謝謝您的來信。我們計畫賠償我們造成的損失如下：

（1）此後一年免費升級您的經濟艙到商務艙。

（2）雙倍旅程積點。

我們希望再次贏得您這樣的一位乘客。我們也真心希望再次為您服務，因此，未來如果您有任何需要請隨時聯繫我們。

真誠地，
瑪麗・史密斯

 重點單字記起來，寫信回信超精準

① **disappointed** adj. 令人失望的
I am so disappointed at my brother's behavior.
→我對弟弟的行為感到非常失望。

② **assign** v. 指派、分派
I was assigned to ICU for three months.
→我被指派到加護病房三個月。

Unit 02 | 行李遺失投訴

想投訴**行李丟失**時，該怎麼寫呢？

Dear Sir or Madam:

This is to complain about a missing **luggage**. I was a passenger in your flight of number NY694 **enroute** from Boston to Taipei on 6 of April, 2020. When arriving inTaipei International Airport, I found that one piece of my luggage was lost.

For your reference, I attached a copy of the Loss Claim Receipt **registered** and issued by your service counter representative.

Please take a look into the matter immediately. I am expecting to receive my luggage and your explanation.

Yours truly,
Min Wang

親愛的先生／女士：

這是關於在您的航班上遺失行李的投訴。2020年4月6日我搭乘你們NY694航班，從波士頓到台北國際機場。在到達台北國際機場時，我發現我的一件行李遺失了。

便於你們參考，我附上了你們服務櫃檯出具的遺失聲明登記和條款。

請儘快處理此事。我期待找回我的行李和你們的解釋。

真誠地，

王敏

收到**行李遺失投訴**信時，該怎麼回呢？ — □ ×

Dear Miss Wang,

Please accept our sincerest apologies. We will look into the matter and find your luggage immediately. As soon as we found your luggage, we will send it to you at once. Meanwhile, we would like to express our appreciation of your letter, it gave a chance to take a look on our working process and find a solution to improve it.

Best regards,
Karen Jensen

親愛的王小姐：

請接受我們誠摯的道歉。我們將立即檢查所有事宜，並尋找您的行李。一旦找到您的行李，我們將馬上快遞給您。同時，我們非常感謝您的來信，給我們一次機會去檢查我們的工作流程，找到解決方案並改善。

真誠地，
卡倫・詹森

不同的答覆還可以怎麼回呢？ — □ ×

Dear Miss Wang,

We are awfully sorry for the trouble this has caused. After our investigation, we found out that another passenger from the same flight you took picked up your suitcase wrongly. As he was on a business trip again, he will send it back to us on this Monday, and we will transport it to you as soon as we received it.

Sorry again.

Best regards,
Karen Jensen

Chapter
2

Part 1
Part 2
意外插曲 Accidents

Part 3
Part 4

親愛的王小姐：

我們為我們給您帶來的不便感到非常抱歉。經過調查，我們發現另外一個同機的旅客錯拿了您的行李。由於他又出差了，這週一他會把行李替我們送回來。我們一收到會立刻快遞給您。

再次抱歉。

真誠地，

卡倫・詹森

重點單字記起來，寫信回信超精準

① **luggage** n. 行李
They lost all of their luggage at the bus station.
→他們在公車站弄丟所有行李。

② **en route** ph. 在途中
Unfortunately, the transportation stopped en route from Taipei to Taichung.
→不幸的是，運輸在台北往台中的路上停止了。

③ **register** v. 註冊、申報、登記
Can I have the mail registered?
→我能用掛號郵寄這封信嗎？

④ **improve** v. 改善、改進、進步
The team's academic performance is surely improving.
→團隊的學術表現確實正在進步。

Unit 03 | 宿舍電路故障

想投訴**電路服務**時，確認信該怎麼寫呢？

Dear Floor Supervisor,

I am sending this letter to complain about **electricity** service of our building. It has been the fifth time in this month that we suffered the **blackout** and the electricity power **interruption** is getting longer and longer. As it is our exam period, this issue has been seriously bothering us on the preparation. Hope this issue can be resolved quickly

Sincerely,

Maria Dowling

親愛的大樓管理員：

我寫這封信給您是投訴本大樓的電路服務。這已經是這個月第5次我們遭受停電了，而且停電時間持續越來越長了。正值考期，這個問題嚴重的干擾了我們的考試準備。希望此問題能盡快解決。

誠摯地，

瑪利亞・道琳

Chapter
2

Part 1

Part 2

意外插曲 Accidents

Part 3

Part 4

收到**投訴電路服務**的信時，該怎麼回呢？　— □ ✕

Dear Miss Dowling,

We are terribly sorry for the electricity power issue and we are working on it. It's just that the component for the **replacement** of an old pipe just arrived in this morning. We will try our best to solve the problem by tomorrow.

Regards,

Eddie Collins

親愛的道琳小姐：

我們對電力問題深感抱歉，我們正在處理。只是替換舊水管的零件今早才剛送到，我們會盡量在明天前修好。

真誠地，

埃迪・柯斯琳

不同的答覆還可以怎麼回呢？　— □ ✕

Dear Miss Dowling,

Please allow us to send you our sincerest apologies. I promise we will solve the problem by tomorrow afternoon. Sorry again for the trouble we brought, and we wish you succeed in your exam.

Best regards,

Eddie Collins

親愛的道琳：

請允許我們送上誠摯的歉意。我保證明天下午解決問題。再次為我們給你們帶來的不便深表歉意，祝你們金榜題名。

誠摯地，

埃迪・柯斯琳

重點單字 記起來，寫信回信超精準

① **electricity** n. 電、電流、電力
The electricity was cut off because we didn't pay the bill. →因為我們沒繳費，電被切斷了。

② **blackout** ph. 停電
I was stuck in the elevatior during the blackout.
→停電時，我被困在電梯裡。

③ **interruption** n. 阻擾、阻礙、干擾
The rain continued for a whole week without interruption.
→雨整週下不停。

④ **replacement** n. 取代、替換、更換
Our department is in an urgent need of a replacement for an accountant.
→我們部門極需一名替補會計人員。

Unit 04 | 申請更換房間

Ms. Lively,

I'd like to know when I can move to a single room that I apply for at the very beginning of the semester. Now I'm living with my roommate. We have absolutely **opposite** living habits, so it's quite hard for us to live together.

For example, she needs to sleep with all lights on, which could totally drive me nuts!I can hardly sleep and have **suffered from** insomnia for almost two weeks. Moreover, she needs to set roughly eight alarm clocks to wake her up every morning, but never turns them off immediately, just letting them ring for more than 5 minutes…

I wonder if you can help arrange the dorm by the end of this month, and provide the details about the payment. Thank you in advance.

Henry Tien

萊佛莉小姐，

我想知道我何時能夠搬進我在學期初申請的單人宿舍呢？我現在與我室友同住，但我們的生活習慣完全相反，我們真的很難同住一房。

舉例來說，她睡覺時需要打開所有的燈，簡直要逼瘋我！這讓我難以入睡且深受失眠之苦長達兩週。還有，她每天早上需要八個鬧鐘叫她起床，但每次響了也不馬上關掉，就讓鬧鐘大響超過五分鐘……

我想知道您是否可在本月底前幫忙安排宿舍，並提供我付款細節，先謝謝你了！

田亨利

收到**更換房間**的申請信時，該怎麼回呢？   — ☐ ✕

Mr. Tien,

There will be a single room available by next month. I can keep it for you. Please bring your student ID card to my office to finish the registration in person. I'll provide more details then. Thank you.

Jennifer Lively

田同學，

本月底前會有一間空的單人房，我可以幫你保留。請攜帶你的學生證親自到我辦公室完成登記，屆時將提供你更多資訊，謝謝。

珍妮佛・萊佛莉

不同的答覆還可以怎麼回呢？   — ☐ ✕

Hi Tien,

Sorry to inform you that all the single rooms are already booked this semester. It was arranged in **registration sequence**. Please refer to the website below and fill in the sheet. Once there's any vacancy in this semester, you will get the notification.

Jennifer Lively

嗨田同學，

很抱歉告知你，本學期的單人房都已被預約，這是按照登記順序安排的。請參閱下方網頁並完成表單填寫，一旦有空房釋出你就會收到通知。

珍妮佛・萊佛莉

Chapter 2

Part 1

Part 2

意外插曲 Accidents

Part 3

Part 4

重點單字記起來，寫信回信超精準

① **opposite** adj. 相反的、截然不同的、迥異的
We have completely opposite personal traits.
→我們的人格特質大相徑庭。

② **suffer from** v. 受……之苦、受……折磨
He's been suffering from asthma for more than ten years. →他受氣喘之苦已經超過十年了。

③ **registration** n. 註冊、登記
Before entering the gym, he's asked to fill out the registration form.
→進入健身房前，他被要求填寫一份登記表格。

④ **sequence** n. 順序、前後、次序
He arranged the shipping in ordering sequence.
→他依照訂單順序安排出貨。

Unit 01 | 申請變更主修

想**申請轉換主修**時，該怎麼寫呢？

Dear Dean of Academic Affairs,

My name is Min Wang. I have been enrolled in our university since last September in a master program of International Law. Unfortunately, I feel that I am not interested in this subject and I prefer Commercial Law to international law. Therefore, I would like to apply for the master program of Commercial Law.

I have studied International Law for one academic year and I would also like to **waiver** the **credits** of this subject to my subject of Commercial Law as well.

Thanks in advance for your consideration on my application. I am looking forward to your approval.

Sincerely Yours,
Min Wang

尊敬的教務長：

我叫王敏，我自去年9月入學，學習國際法學碩士課程。很不幸，我感覺我對這個專業並沒有興趣，而對商事法更感興趣。因此，我想申請轉系到商事法專業的碩士學習。

我已修讀國際法一學年，也希望申請將我已修得的學分轉到商事法專業。

非常感謝您對我的申請予以考慮。期待能儘快收到您的回覆。

真誠地，
王敏

Chapter
2

Part 1
Part 2
Part 3
Part 4

求學之路 Studying process

收到學生**申請變更主修**的信時，該怎麼回呢？ — □ ×

Dear Min,

For the application on transferring your major from International Law to Commercial Law, we decided to give our approval, along with your credit transfer. Please bring your student card and **transcript** to the registration office to go through the **formalities**.

If you have any further inquiries, please feel free to contact me.

Yours sincerely,

Kate Ross

親愛的王敏同學：

針對你的自國際法轉到商事法的轉系申請，我們決定批准你的轉系和轉移學分的申請。請攜帶你的學生證及學習成績單，到本校學科登記辦公室去辦理相關手續。

如有任何問題，請再與我聯繫。

真誠地，

凱特‧羅斯

不同的答覆還可以怎麼回呢？ — □ ×

Dear Min,

As Commercial Law class is fully registered, I am sorry to inform you that your application is not approved.

Please feel free to contact me if you have any other inquiries.

Yours sincerely,

Kate Ross

親愛的王敏同學：

由於商業法學班已經滿員，我不得不遺憾地通知你，你的申請沒被批准透過。

如有其他任何問題，請再與我聯繫。

真誠地，

凱特‧羅斯

 重點單字記起來，寫信回信超精準

① **waiver** v. 轉讓、棄權
It is up to each individual department to decide the number of credits a student may waiver.
→學生轉讓的學分是由個別系所決定的。

② **credit** n. 學分、信譽、帳款
I still have 30 credits to earn.
→我還有30個學分要修。

③ **transcript** n. 成績單、副本
I failed the exam so I hid the transcript from my parents. →我考試不及格所以把成績單藏起來不讓爸媽看到。

④ **formality** n. 正式程序、拘謹
It is a formality to go to the registration office first.
→先去註冊組是正式程序。

Unit 02 | 必修學分標準

想詢問需要修**多少學分**時，該怎麼寫呢？

Ms. Choo,

I'm now selecting courses and I'd like to know what **compulsory** credits to obtain as a senior. It's because I'm planning to apply for student exchange to Germany for one year after this semester. I'd like to select some compulsory credits for a senior student in advance so that I won't have a tight schedule after coming back as I want to apply for an intern job before I graduate.

I know some professors do not allow a junior student to select senior courses, but I could write to them to **interpret**. Lastly, could you please provide information about the required graduation **threshold**?

Thank you!
Ariel

丘小姐，

我目前正在選課，我想知道大四學生需要哪些必修學分？因為我正計劃本學期結束後要前往德國成為交換學生一年，我想預先選些大四學生的課，這樣我回國後行程才不會太過緊湊，因為我想在畢業前申請實習工作。

我知道有些教授不願意讓大三學生提前修大四的課，但我可以寫信向他們解釋。最後，請問您可以提供我關於畢業門檻的資訊嗎？

謝謝！
愛瑞兒

Hi Ariel,

To earn a Bachelor's Degree, you must complete a major, meet the academic standard, and pass English Proficiency Test. You can refer to the official department website for details. Please note that it is your **responsibility** to be aware of requirements and complete them. Feel free to ask if there's any doubt and concern.

Regards,

Choo

嗨愛瑞兒，

要取得學士學位，首先你得要完成一個主修，達到學科標準，並通過英文能力測驗。你可以到系上官網參閱詳細資料。

請注意，留意這些必要條件並完成是你的責任哦！有任何疑慮歡迎隨時提出！

誠摯地，

丘

Hi Ariel,

Indeed, there're some cases that junior students take seniors' courses.

To do so, you need to attend an exam to see if you're qualified to take advanced courses. I'd like to confirm with your advisor first. After that, I'll inform you to come to the department office to fill in the application form. I'll get back to you soon.

Best wishes,

Choo

Chapter

2

Part 1
Part 2
Part 3
Part 4

求學之路 Studying process

嗨愛瑞兒，

的確，有些案例是大三學生修大四學生的課程。

如果要這樣做的話，你需要參加測驗確認你符合選修進階課程的資格。

我會先跟你的顧問確認，在那之後我會通知你到系辦公室填寫申請表格，我盡快回覆你。

真誠地，

丘

 重點單字記起來，寫信回信超精準

① **compulsory** adj. 義務性的、強制性的
Taiwan government makes masks compulsory on public transportation because of the spread of Covid-19. →台灣政府因新冠肺炎的傳播，強制規定搭乘大眾運輸交通工具需配戴口罩。

② **interpret** v. 理解、說明、闡述
It's difficult to interpret this report without any background knowledge. →沒有背景知識很難說明這份報告。

③ **threshold** n. 門檻、水準、界線
He earns US$3500 a month to meet the threshold of making ends meet for a big family which consists of 10 members. →他月入3500美金來維持十人家庭收支平衡的門檻。

④ **responsibility** n. 職責、責任
Kelly considers that taking good care of all family members is the responsibility as a mother.
→凱莉認為照顧好家中每一位成員是作為一位母親的責任。

Unit 03 | 期末報告討論

想和組員進行期末報告討論時，該怎麼寫呢？ ─ □ ✕

Dear all,

The final presentation of Western Literature Analysis is right on the corner. I'd like to know if everyone's **available** on this Saturday afternoon? I've reserved a discussion room on 5th floor of T4 Building. Please bring your laptops and literature review. Be on time so that we could make it efficiently. If you cannot be in that day, please let me know. Thank you!

Regards,

Helen

親愛的各位，

西洋文學分析的期末報告要到啦！我想請問大家這週六下午有沒有空？我預約了T4大樓五樓的討論室，請帶著你們的電腦跟文獻資料來，請準時抵達我們才能有效率地進行，如果你當天不能出席，請先讓我知道，謝謝！

誠摯地，

海倫

Chapter

2

Part 1

Part 2

Part 3

求學之路 Studying process

Part 4

收到要**討論期末報告**的信時，該怎麼回呢？ — □ ×

Morning Helen,

So nice to work with you and thanks for the arrangement. I'd like to know what time we'll start the meeting. I have an **appointment** with my doctor on that day. I'll check if I need to rearrange my schedule. Feel free to contact me when the time's confirmed. Thank you again.

Anna

早安海倫！

很高興跟你一組也謝謝你的安排。我想知道我們幾點會開始討論？我當天跟醫生預約了門診，我要確認我是否要重新安排我當天行程，時間確認後可隨時跟我聯絡，再次感謝！

安娜

不同的答覆還可以怎麼回呢？ — □ ×

Hi Helen,

I'm afraid that I cannot be in the meeting since I won't be in Taipei next Wednesday. My little sister's cello **debut** will take place on next Wednesday in Taichung, and all my family members are invited to the concert. I don't want to miss out the special moment in her life. I wonder if we can change the meeting time to next Tuesday or Thursday? If no, could you please pass the details to me after the meeting? I **apologize** for causing any inconvenience to you.

Anna

嗨海倫！

我當天可能無法參與，因為我下週三不在台北。下週三我妹妹將在台中出演她的大提琴初登場，所有家人都受邀了，我不想錯過她生命中如此特別的時刻！我想知道我們能改到下週二或下週四嗎？如果不行的話，你可以在會議後傳達細節給我嗎？造成你的困擾真的很抱歉！

安娜

重點單字記起來，寫信回信超精準

① **available** adj. 可取得的、有空的
Is there coffee shop around here?
→這附近有咖啡店嗎？

② **appointment** n. 預約、約會、約定
I need to drive my grandma to the clinic for her appointment with her dentist.
→我需要載我奶奶到診所，因為她有預約牙醫。

③ **debut** n. 初登場、首次演出
Shelley must be quite nervous now because it's her debut as an actress.
→薛莉現在一定很緊張，因為這是她作為女演員的初登場。

④ **apologize** v. 道歉、致歉
I sincerely apologize for my recklessness.
→我為我的魯莽道歉。

Unit 04｜上課事前請假

想要和老師**提前請假**時，該怎麼寫呢？

Ms. Lee,

I'd like to ask for sick leave for next Wed's class. I have not been feeling well these days. I had a fever and felt dizzy after I went mountain climbing with friends last weekend. I've already made the reservation for health check, so will be absent for next week's class. As for the midterm reports, I'll send it to you via mail by next Tuesday. Sorry for causing any inconvenient. Thank you!

Best wishes,

Catie

李老師，

我下週三的課需要請病假，我這幾天身體不適，上週末跟朋友去爬山之後有發燒及暈眩症狀。我已經預約了身體檢查，所以會缺席下週的課。關於期中報告，我下週二前會透過信件寄給您，很抱歉對您造成任何困擾，謝謝。

真誠地，

凱蒂

Catie,

Hope you get well soon.

No worries about the midterm report. Just sent it to me when you're feeling better. As I remember, students need to select the courses online next Wednesday morning. If you cannot make it due to the health check, don't forget to ask the department office for an alternative. Take care!

Regards,

Lee

凱蒂：

希望你早日康復。

不用擔心期中報告，你身體好點之後再寄給我就好。印象中學生下週三早上要選課，如果你因為健康檢查沒辦法處理的話，記得要到系辦公室尋求其他解決辦法，保重！

真誠地，

李

Hi Catie,

Your attendance rate is quite poor as you've already took many days off in this semester. You need to check if you meet the standard of attendance rate standard or you will fail the course. Take good care of yourself.

Best wishes,

Lee

Chapter
2

Part 1

Part 2

Part 3

求學之路 Studying process

Part 4

嗨凱蒂，

你這學期因為已經請太多假而出席率超低，你要留意自己是否達到出席門檻，否則這門課就會被當掉哦！好好保重。

真誠地，

李

 重點單字記起來，寫信回信超精準

① **sick leave** ph. 病假
He asked for sick leave for serious allergy.
→他因為嚴重過敏而請病假。

② **absent** adj. 缺席的、缺勤的
Benny's been absent from school for 3 days.
→班尼已經曠課三天了。

③ **alternative** n. 解決辦法、兩者擇一的選擇/辦法
There's no alternative for this case.
→這個案子沒有其他辦法。

④ **attendance** n. 參加、出席
The flu made poor school attendance rate.
→流感導致上課出席率很低。

Unit 05 | 詢問補考事宜

想要詢問**補考事宜**時，該怎麼寫呢？　　　─ □ ✕

Prof.Hung,

Due to my severe **abdominal pain**, I was absent from the midterm exam yesterday. I'd like to know if there's any possibility to take make-up exam? I don't want to fail it at all. I've been preparing for it for so long. I can't fail any exam as I've already applied for scholarships to pay for my tuition. If I failed, I will not be **qualified** to apply for them.

I know you will not be in Taiwan for around two weeks for academic conference. If necessary, I can visit your office and talk to you in person. Any time is fine for me. Sincerely waiting for your reply. Thank you.

Best regards,

Ben

洪教授，

我昨日因腹部劇烈疼痛而缺席期中考試。我想了解是否有補考的可能性？我完全不想搞砸這科，我已為此準備了好久。我不能搞砸任何一科考試，因為我申請了獎學金以支付我的學費。如果我被當，我就沒有資格申請這些獎學金了。

我知道您將出席學術會議而有兩週不在台灣，如果需要的話，我可親自到您辦公室跟您談談，任何時間皆可行。誠摯等候您的回覆，謝謝。

真誠地，

班

Chapter
2

Part 1
Part 2
Part 3
Part 4

求學之路 Studying process

收到學生詢問補考的信時，該**怎麼回**呢？　— □ ✕

Hi Ben,

I totally understand your situation.

Sure. Make-up exam works. Please come to my office at 3p.m. this Friday. My assistant will give you midterm exam sheet. Of course. It's Sheet B, which is totally different from the one that students took yesterday. After finishing, just hand in your exam paperto her. Remember that this is the only **opportunity** for make-up exam because I need to upload all your grades to the system by this Saturday night. If you can't make it on this Friday, must let me know before tomorrow morning. Take care.

Yours sincerely,
Hung

嗨班，

我完全理解你的狀況。

當然！補考沒有問題，請在本週五下午三點來我辦公室，我的助理會給你期中考卷，當然這是B卷，跟昨天學生寫的那份完全不同，你寫完後只需將試卷交給助理。請記得這是你唯一的補考機會，因為週六晚上以前我必須將你們的所有成績上傳至系統上，如果這週五你不能來，請在明天早上以前告知我，保重。

誠摯地，
洪

不同的答覆還可以怎麼回呢？　— □ ✕

Ben,

As I know, there's no make-up exam for students who didn't **show up** in the midterm. Considering your situation, I'll ask the director to see if there's any solution. No worries and rest well. I'll send you email to inform you if any alternative provided.

All the best,
Hung

班，

就我所知，缺考學生並沒有補考機會，但考量你的情況，我會詢問主任是否有任何解決辦法。別擔心，好好休息，如果有替代作法我會透過郵件通知你。

真誠地，

洪

 重點單字記起來，寫信回信超精準

① **abdominal pain** ph. 腹痛
The doctor still cannot find out what caused Tim's abdominal pain. →醫生仍查不出提姆腹痛的原因。

② **qualify** v. 使合格、使具備資格
She qualified as a pilot last year.
→她去年成為了一名合格的機師。

③ **opportunity** n. 機會
She was never given an opportunity to meet her father. →她從來沒有機會見她的父親。

④ **show up** ph. 出現、現身、出席、揭露
Sam didn't show up until the end of the ceremony.
→山姆直到典禮結束才出現。

Unit 06 | 申請校外實習

Mr. Yen,

Hope this mail finds you well.

This is Daisy, a senior from Department of Hotel Management, BC University.

R Hotel, **ranked** as the 10 best hotels among Asia, is always an enterprise I want to be a part of. And that's why I apply for the intern position job today. I've worked as an intern in ZX Hotel when I was a sophomore, gaining lots of **precious** experience in working in a hotel. Apart from my experience, I also learn English, Japanese, and Thai at the same time, getting certificates of comprehension tests, which makesme be able to communicate with customers from worldwide.

With my experience and passion, I'm confident that I'm ready for the intern position. I sincerely hope that I could join the big team and devote what I have learned to the industry I deeply love.

I'm looking forward to hearing from you. Thank you!

Daisy

....

顏先生，

收信愉快！

我是來自BC大學飯店管理系的大四學生黛西，亞洲排名前十的R飯店一直是我想加入的企業，這也是我申請實習機會的原因，大二的時候我曾在ZX飯店當過實習生，累積了許多寶貴的經驗。除了上述提及，我也學習英語、日語、泰語，並拿到語言證書，這也讓我得以跟來自世界各地的貴賓溝通。

憑藉我的經驗與熱情，我很自信我已做好擔任實習的準備了！誠摯希望能夠加入這個大團隊，並且將我所學奉獻給我熱愛的產業。

期待您的回覆，謝謝！

黛西

收到校外實習的申請信時，該**怎麼回**呢？　— ☐ ✕

Hi Daisy,

First of all, thank you for applying for the intern position job.

Honestly speaking, we're quite impressed by your CV and the interview, which totally showed how well-prepared you are for this job. As the spirit we stick to all the way: "We go together to go far," we'd like to find a teammate that shares the same core concept with us, and we're glad and excited to have you in our big team! Go explore and have fun in the following 6 months! It's going to be an interesting and **unforgettable** journey in your life.

Regards,

Yen

嗨黛西，

首先，感謝你申請實習職缺。

老實說，我們對於你的履歷及面試都印象深刻，在在顯現你為了這個工作做了多完善的準備。就像我們一路以來堅持的精神：「一群人走很遠。」我們希望能夠找到一個跟我們有同樣核心理念的夥伴，而對於你能夠加入我們這個大團隊，我們感到非常開心且興奮！未來六個月盡情探索、玩得開心！這一定會是你生命中一次有趣且難忘的旅程！

真誠地，

顏

Chapter
2

Part 1
Part 2
Part 3

求學之路 Studying process

Part 4

不同的答覆 還可以怎麼回呢？ — □ ✕

Daisy,

Thanks for having interests in R Hotel. It's our pleasure.

However, I'm sorry to inform you that we have already selected the intern partner, and he will report next Monday. You are on the standby list #1. Once he didn't report to the office then, we will inform you. Thank you.

All the best,
Yen

黛西，

感謝你對R飯店這麼感興趣，這是我們的榮幸。

然而很抱歉地告知您，我們已經選出實習夥伴，他下週一會報到。你是我們候補名單上的第一位，如果他屆時沒有報到的話，我們將會通知您，謝謝。

誠摯地，
顏

 重點單字 記起來，寫信回信超精準

① **rank** v. 排名、評等
In my point of view, Jennifer ranks among the greatest movie actresses. →就我的觀點而言，珍妮佛是電影女演員中的佼佼者。

② **precious** adj. 珍寶的、寶貴的
Her little boy is undoubtedly precious to her.
→她小兒子無疑是她的珍寶。

③ **unforgettable** adj. 難忘的
The days of working holiday in Canada is unforgettable to me. →在加拿大打工度假日子對我而言很難忘。

Unit 01 | 論文通過審核

想祝賀對方通過**論文審核**時，該怎麼寫呢？

Dear Min,

Congratulations on the success of passing your **dissertation** defense. We all knew that Professor Smith is **strict** in the quality of dissertation, so if someone passed his subject, he/she must be very good.

Therefore, we decided to hold a celebration for you. If you have time tomorrow evening, I will ask David, Jack, and Wilson to go to Lotus Restaurant and have a Chinese dinner. What do you think?

Looking forward to hearing from you.

Regards,

Alex

親愛的敏：

恭喜你成功通過論文口試了。我們都知道史密斯教授對於論文品質要求嚴格，如果能通過了他的科目，這個人必定非常棒。

所以我們決定幫你慶祝一下。如果明天晚上你有時間，我將邀請大衛，傑克和威爾士到荷花餐廳，享用中國菜。你覺得怎麼樣？

期待你的回覆。

誠摯地，

艾力克斯

Chapter 2

Part 1
Part 2
Part 3
Part 4

順利畢業 Graduating

收到**祝賀論文通過**的信時，該怎麼回呢？   — ☐ ✕

Dear Alex,

Thanks for your letter and suggestion. I would love to have a Chinese dinner with you guys. I definitely think I deserve a night out it after months of hard work on the dissertation. Let's meet tomorrow evening at 18:00 in Lotus Restaurant.

Sincerely,

Min

親愛的艾力克斯：

感謝你的來信和建議，我很高興與你們一起享用中國菜。經過數月的努力我想確實值得出去慶祝。那麼我們明天晚上6點在荷花餐廳見面。

真誠地，

敏

不同的答覆還可以怎麼回呢？   — ☐ ✕

Dear Alex,

Thanks for your letter. It was not easy to pass the dissertation as Professor Smith is indeed a **demanding** teacher. During the process of writing the dissertation, I got **frustrated** from time to time. Finally, I passed it!

How about postponing the celebration to the day after tomorrow? I have an important appointment tomorrow evening. Hope you don't mind. Also, please also invite Steve. He gave me a lot of help when I was struggling for the dissertation.

Please let me know if it is ok.

Best wishes,

Min

親愛的艾力克斯：

感謝你的來信。要通過論文確實不容易，因為史密斯教授真的是一位要求嚴格的老師。在寫論文的過程中，有時候我會特別沮喪。最後，我通過了！

我們後天慶祝如何？明天晚上我還有一個重要的約會。希望你不介意。以及，請邀請史蒂夫一同前來，我寫論文遇到困難時他也給了我很多幫助。

如果你們可以請通知我。

誠摯地，

敏

 重點單字 記起來，寫信回信超精準

① **dissertation** n 論文、畢業（或學位）論文
He finished hisdoctoral dissertation within only two months. →他在兩個月內便完成了他的博士論文。

② **strict** adj 嚴格的、嚴厲的、絕對的
My mother is very strict with our upbringing.
→我媽媽對我們的教養非常嚴謹。

③ **demanding** adj 要求高的、苛求的
The professor was not only demanding but also arrogant.
→那位教授不僅要求高，還很傲慢。

④ **frustrated** adj 挫敗的、失意的、洩氣的
He felt so frustrated after he failed the exam more than five times. →在考試失利五次之後他感到非常受挫。

Unit 02 | 得到獎學金

想祝福對方申請到**獎學金**時，該怎麼寫呢？ ─ □ ✕

Dear Tracy,

Congratulations! Today is the day you received a scholarship from Boston University and such a **scholarship represents** your **qualification** to enter the master program there. Your experience encourages all students who study hard, and it also opened a door for your bright future. I wish you achieve all your targets in future.

Yours sincerely,

Amy

親愛的特蕾西：

恭喜你！今天你收到了波士頓大學的獎學金，這個獎學金也代表著你能到那裡修習碩士課程的資格。你的經歷鼓舞了所有努力學習的學生，也為你的美好未來開啟了一道門。我希望未來你能實現所有的目標。

誠摯地，

艾米

收到**祝賀自己獲得獎學金**的信時，該怎麼回呢？ — □ ✕

Dear Amy,

Thanks for your letter. This is a big reward for me and it encourages me to further achieve my next goal. I am looking forward for my new life in Boston. Also, without your help, I couldn't have made it this far. I wish you the best, too.

Sincerely,

Tracy

親愛的艾米：

謝謝你的來信。這對我是極大的回報，並鼓舞我去接著實現下一個目標。我期待我在波士頓的新生活。以及，沒有你的幫助，我也不可能走到這裡。我也希望你一切都好。

真誠地，

特蕾西

不同的答覆還可以怎麼回呢？ — □ ✕

Dear Amy,

Much gratitude for your letter. This scholarship is a big reward and helps me continue to **chase** my dream in Boston. I believe that in this new stage, I will gain more knowledge and have a wonderful experience in my student life.

Thanks again and I wish you all the best, too.

Regards,

Tracy

Chapter
2

Part 1
Part 2
Part 3
Part 4

順利畢業 Graduating

親愛的艾米：

感謝你的來信。這個獎學金對我是極大的回報並能幫助我在波士頓繼續追逐我的夢想。我相信在新的階段。我能學到更多知識而且在我的學生生活裡會有一個精彩的經歷。

再次感謝，也希望你一切都好。

真誠地，

特蕾西

 重點單字 記起來，寫信回信超精準

① **scholarship** n. 獎學金
Eventually, he won a scholarship to the prestigious university.
→終於，他獲得了去那間聲望極佳的大學讀書的獎學金。

② **represent** v. 代表、表示
I represent my boss to send my condolences.
→我代表我的老闆以示哀悼。

③ **qualification** n. 資格、能力
The athlete failed to pass the qualification for the annual championship.
→那名運動員未能獲得參加年度錦標賽的資格。

④ **chase** v. 追逐、追蹤、追求
My sister continued to chase after her dream as a District Attorney.
→我妹妹持續追求成為地區檢察官的夢想。

Unit 03 | 祝福順利畢業

想祝福他人**順利畢業**時，該怎麼寫呢？

Dear Robin,

Congratulations! After four yearsof **diligent** studies, you finally graduated from New York University. Looking back to the first year you joined our university, you were so excited about your student life. I guess you never expected time to run so fast. Now, you have graduated and are going back Sydney, your hometown. I hope such distance will not become an **obstacle** to our friendship, and I wish you a very successful career there.

All the best to you and I am looking forward to seeing you again someday in future.

Sincerely,

John

親愛的羅賓：

恭喜你！經過四年的努力學習，你從紐約大學畢業了。回顧你入學的第一年，你對大學生活是那麼興奮。我猜你從沒意識到時間會過得這麼快。現在，你畢業了，就要回到你的家鄉雪梨了。我希望這樣的距離不會阻隔我們的友誼。祝你事業成功。

祝你一切都好，期待以後再見。

誠摯地，

約翰

Chapter
2

Part 1
Part 2
Part 3
Part 4

順利畢業 Graduating

收到他人祝賀自己順利畢業的信時，該**怎麼回**呢？ — ◻ ✕

Dear John,

Indeed, time flies, and I am leaving for Sydney soon. However, I will keep all the good memories of my student life here in my mind. I will definitely come back to visit our beautiful campus and you someday. Of course, you are very welcome to come to my hometown; I will take you to the best restaurant there. I am also sure that long distance won't be a thing to our friendship. Let's keep in touch.

All the best to you as well, and hope to see you soon in Sydney.

Regards,
Robin

親愛的約翰：

的確，時間過得飛快，我很快要回雪梨了。我將珍藏我們學生生活的所有美好回憶在心裡。某天，我一定回來拜訪我們美麗的校園以及拜訪你。當然，也歡迎你到我的家鄉來。我將帶你去最好的餐館。我也堅信距離對我們友誼來說不會是個問題。保持聯繫。

也祝你一切都好，希望在雪梨見到你。

誠摯地，
羅賓

不同的答覆還可以怎麼回呢？ — ◻ ✕

Dear John,

Thanks for your letter. As people always say, time flies like an arrow, and happy times runs even faster. I feel like it was just yesterday. New York is a **splendid** city and my student life here is just awesome! I cannot imagine where else I can have such fun.

I hope you can visit me in Sydney someday and of course, I will come back to visit you, too. Living in an era of technology, we can make our friendship last for sure.

I wish you all the best and looking forward to seeing you in Sydney soon.

Sncerely,

Robin

親愛的約翰：

感謝你的來信。的確像人們常說的，時光飛逝，快樂的時光過得更是特別快。感覺就像昨天一樣。紐約是一個美麗的城市，我的學生生活在這裡很棒！我無法想像在其他地方能如此快樂。

我希望某天，你可以到雪梨來看我，當然我也會回來看你的。活在科技時代，我們絕對可以使友誼長存。

我也希望你一切都安好，期待很快能在雪梨見到你。

誠摯地，

羅賓

 重點單字 記起來，寫信回信超精準

① **diligent** `adj.` 勤奮的、勤勉的
I have always been a diligent student since I was little. →我從小時候開始就一直是個很用功的學生。

② **obstacle** `n.` 障礙（物）、妨礙
His sentimentality has become an obstacle to every teamwork for him. →他的多愁善感成為他進行團隊工作的障礙。

③ **splendid** `adj.` 極好的、令人極其滿意的
Her splendid memory earned her a good reputation in the oral interpretation field. →她絕佳的記憶力使她在口譯界享負盛名。

Unit 04 | 恭賀學生畢業

想恭賀**學生畢業**時，該怎麼寫呢？　　

Dear Min,

On behalf of all the faculty in Tainan University, I would like to sincerely congratulate you on your graduation with your Bachelor Degree in Law. I have **anticipated** this moment with full **confidence** as you are one of our best students. During your first year in our university, I noted how diligent you are and how bright you were with a quick mind. Considering those **perspectives**, it is obvious that you have a promising future ahead of you.

I wish you all the best in your future.

Yours sincerely,

Ming Ma

親愛的敏：

我代表台南大學的所有教職員，真誠的祝福你取得了法律學士學位。我已經預料到在此刻作為我們最好的學生之一，你充滿了信心。你入學的第一年，我就注意到你有多認真而且你反應有多快。綜合各方面，在你面前的將會是美好的未來。

代表我們學校，祝福你未來一切都好。

誠摯地，

馬明

Dear Ming,

Thanks for your kind letter. I am happy and proud to graduate from Tainan University. I now have four years of the happiest time in my life, and I met the nicest faculty and classmates during this phase.

I will keep working hard in the future. All the best to you, too.

Yours sincerely,

Min

親愛的明：

感謝您的來信。能從台南大學畢業我感到很高興而且自豪。在這裡我度過了愉快的四年時光，且我遇到了最好的老師和同學。這些經歷將成為我生命中最最寶貴的財富。

我將繼續努力工作。也祝你一切順利。

誠摯地，

敏

不同的答覆還可以怎麼回呢？ — □ ✕

Dear Ming,

Thanks for your kind letter. Entering Tainan University and graduating from here was always my dream when I was a teenager. I can say I am proud of living this dream now and I feel like the luckiest person in the world. In the past four years, I received the best education and formed friendships with whom I will now call my best friends. All these will be my best treasure, and I'll continue to work hard in the future.

Yours sincerely,

Min

Chapter

2

Part 1
Part 2
Part 3
Part 4

順利畢業 Graduating

親愛的明：

感謝您的來信。能進入台南大學並從這裡畢業是我少年時的夢想。現在，我能自豪地說，我實現了這個夢想，並覺得自己是這個世界上最幸運的人。過去的四年，在這裡我接受了最好的教育而且認識了我現在會稱為摯友的人，這些都將是我最寶貴的財富，在未來我也會繼續認真努力。

誠摯地，

敏

 **重點單字**記起來，寫信回信超精準

① **on behalf of** ph. 代表
No one can sign the contract on behalf of me.
→沒有人可以代替我簽這份合約。

② **anticipate** v. 預期、期望、預料
All the students are anticipating the coming of the outing. →所有學生都很期待戶外教學的到來。

③ **confidence** n. 信心、信任
Lack of confidence is the main reason why he failed the interview. →缺乏自信心是他面試失敗的主因。

④ **perspective** n. 觀點、展望
We should try to see the good in all perspectives and reach a conclusion. →我們應擷取所有觀點的好處並達成結論。

Unit 05 | 錄取研究身份

想恭喜對方**錄取研究所**時，該怎麼寫呢？ ⊟ □ ✕

Dear Max,

I am very happy to learn that you have successfully received the offer from Oxford University. Please accept my sincere congratulations on this **occasion** that you have been **admitted** into Oxford University. You have been studying so hard and you got high marks in almost all the subjects. I am really proud of you and firmly believe that you will have a greater success in future.

Yours sincerely,

Mike

親愛的麥克斯：

我很高興聽説你收到牛津大學的錄取通知書。在此請接受我誠摯的祝賀你被牛津大學錄取。你一直認真學習而且所有科目成績優秀。我真為你感到驕傲，我堅信你在未來一定會更成功。

誠摯地，

麥克

Chapter
2

Part 1
Part 2
Part 3
Part 4

順
利
畢
業 Graduating

收到**恭賀自己錄取研究所**的信時，該怎麼回呢？ — □ ✕

Dear Mike,

Thanks for your letter. I am alsovery **delighted** to get the offer. I look forward to my new student life in Oxford.

Also, I knew deep down that my achievement roots from your **encouragement** and support. I hereby express my sincerest gratitude to you. In the future, I will keep working hard and chasing my goal. Wish me good luck, buddy.

Sincerely,

Max

親愛的麥克：

感謝你的來信。的確我非常高興得到錄取通知書。而且很期待我在牛津的學生生活。

此外，我心裡知道我的成果也都離不開你的鼓勵和支持。在此我也表達我誠摯的感謝。將來，我會努力學習，實現我的目標，祝我好運，兄弟。

真誠地，

麥克斯

不同的答覆還可以怎麼回呢？ — □ ✕

Dear Mike,

Thanks for your letter. I cannot believe that my dream came true. I am so excited. I plan to hold a party this Saturday afternoon in my apartment. I have also invited other friends you know. Please come and celebrate my success with us. We will definitely have a lot of fun.

Sincerely,

Max

親愛的麥克：

感謝你的來信。我簡直不能相信我的夢想實現了。我非常興奮。我計畫這週六下午在我的公寓舉辦一個派對。我還邀請了其他你認識的朋友。請和我們一起慶祝吧。我們一定會玩得很盡興。

誠摯地，

麥克斯

 重點單字記起來，寫信回信超精準

① **occasion** n. 場合、時機、時刻
He rose to the occasion and won the competition.
→他隨機應變，贏得比賽。

② **admit** v. 准許進入、承認
All my friends are happy for me after I got admitted to Yale. →我得到耶魯的入學通知時，所有的朋友都替我高興。

③ **delighted** adj. 欣喜的、高興的
I'm sure my parents will be delighted to attend my graduation ceremony.
→我相信我爸媽會很高興參加我的畢業典禮。

④ **encouragement** n. 獎勵、鼓勵
His life story was a huge encouragement to me.
→他的人生故事對我來說是個很大的鼓勵。

Note

原來如此 系列 E233

我的第一本職場 & 出國
萬用 E-mail 攻略

解決職場與出國留學時信件往返疑難雜症，就看這一本！

作　　者	許豪
顧　　問	曾文旭
社　　長	王毓芳
編輯統籌	耿文國、黃璽宇
主　　編	吳靜宜、姜怡安
執行編輯	吳佳芬
美術編輯	王桂芳、張嘉容
封面設計	阿作
法律顧問	北辰著作權事務所　蕭雄淋律師、幸秋妙律師

初　　版	2020 年 09 月
出　　版	捷徑文化出版事業有限公司
電　　話	（02）2752-5618
傳　　真	（02）2752-5619

定　　價	新台幣 320 元／港幣 107 元
產品內容	1 書

總 經 銷	采舍國際有限公司
地　　址	235 新北市中和區中山路二段 366 巷 10 號 3 樓
電　　話	（02）8245-8786
傳　　真	（02）8245-8718

港澳地區總經銷	和平圖書有限公司
地　　址	香港柴灣嘉業街 12 號百樂門大廈 17 樓
電　　話	（852）2804-6687
傳　　真	（852）2804-6409

▶本書圖片由 freepik 圖庫提供。

捷徑 Book站

現在就上臉書（FACEBOOK）「捷徑BOOK站」並按讚加入粉絲團，
就可享每月不定期新書資訊和粉絲專享小禮物喔！

http://www.facebook.com/royalroadbooks
讀者來函：royalroadbooks@gmail.com

國家圖書館出版品預行編目資料

我的第一本職場 & 出國萬用 E-mail 攻略 / 許豪著 . --
初版 . -- 臺北市 : 捷徑文化 , 2020.09
　面；　公分
ISBN 978-986-5507-39-8(平裝)

1. 英語 2. 電子郵件 3. 應用文

805.179　　　　　　　　　　　　　　　109011856